W. P. KINSELLA

BORN INDIAN

"Born Indian" first appeared in *Canadian Fiction Magazine*, "Indian Struck" in *Dandelion*, "The Sisters" in *Martlet Magazine* under the title "Fence & Ermine," "Buffalo Jump" in the *Moosehead Review*, "Goldie" in *Quarry,* "The Chicken Dancer" in *NeWest Review*, "The Runner" in *Edmonton Magazine*, "Suits" in *Canadian Short Fiction Anthology*, "Pretend Dinners," in *Crazy Horse* and *The Pushcart Prize Anthology* 1980 and "Weasels and Ermines" in *Aurora: New Canadian Writing* 80. "The Killing of Colin Moosefeathers was broadcast on CBC *Anthology*.

ISBN 0 88750 379 9 (hardcover)
ISBN 0 88750 381 0 (softcover)

Cover painting by Allen Sapp
Design by Michael Macklem

Printed in Canada

PUBLISHED IN CANADA BY OBERON PRESS

For my daughter Erin Irene

BORN INDIAN

Kingston Oldshoes used to have a wife and daughter. But the daughter, who was named Dora, went off to Edmonton, got swallowed up by the city and it be just the same as if she died. Then his wife really died and he was alone in his cabin that sit in a half-circle of spruce trees about a mile from Blue Quills Dance Hall and what little town of Hobbema there is.

Kingston is crippled some with the arthritis and he walk bent over, held up by a stick, and as if he ain't got no knees. His face is long, sad, about the same colour and about as rough as a potato. He wear a greasy red cap with a long peak, and a green-checked mackinaw that is too big for him. His moccasins show how his feet kind of melted down and flattened out as he got old.

He spend his time sit at the wood table in his cabin, smoke his pipe, drink tea and look out the small window through glasses with blue rims what was gived to him by the Department of Indian Affairs.

Guess he would of stayed that way until he died except one day his daughter come home.

I was there when she step out of the mouth of the south-bound bus in front of Ben Stonebreaker's General Store. I don't know who she is because she went away when I was only a kid. But I find out when she ask if I carry her suitcase for her. She is about 30 and got mean eyes that stare right through you like drill points. That happen to girls who go to the city. A cold wind blowing off the mountains move dirt and papers down the street but Dora Oldshoes wears only jeans and a black T-shirt that say "Disco Till You Drop" in silver letters. She got clutched in her right arm a baby in blue sleepers that is so dirty they look like they been used to wash a floor. The baby is tiny, new and got eyes black as little mud puddles. I see as we walk that Dora got some teeth missing and a couple of bad scars on her face. Her arms and hands have tattoos on them, some been made by a tattoo man, some she done herself with ink and a needle or a jack-knife.

She ain't much for talking.

"How old is the baby?" I ask.

"Two months," she say.

"Where you been living?"

"Edmonton."

"You plan on staying or just visit?"

She look sharp at me out of her eyes that is a dirty yellow around their black centres.

"I was in jail when the baby was born. Welfare tell me I got to come home or they take him away. I figure he was born Indian, we give it one chance here," and she stop and cough loud.

I decide not to ask any more questions.

Kingston Oldshoes don't appear surprised that his daughter come home after maybe ten years.

All he say to her is, "What do you call . . . ?" and he stretch his old brown neck toward the baby what lay in the middle of Kingston's bed, like a five-pointed blue flower on the dark blanket.

"Jonah. Nuns come around say that would be a good

6

name for him."

Dora don't offer to talk about her life in the city and we don't ask. And nobody ever find out because about a month later she get herself killed. Was early on Sunday after a dance at Blue Quills Hall that she got run over by a bunch of white guys in a car. They claim she was playing "chicken" with them on the road to the dance hall, and even some of the Indians who was there say so too. Doctor claim she have enough alcohol in her to make three people drunk.

People are nice to Kingston for a few days: some ladies come around and show him how to take care of Jonah. Then they go back to their own troubles. Most of them got problems worse than Kingston's.

But there are people whose business *is* other people's problems. Government pay them to spy on us Indians.

"They creep around like people who *have* to look in windows," says Kingston, after he been visited by a Welfare lady.

"How do they know to come? They're like birds who eat dead things—who can smell death from a mile in the sky," I say to Mad Etta, our medicine lady, who shrug her buffalo-big shoulders.

The Welfare is worried that Jonah don't have a mama no more and that Kingston too old to care for him. They don't know what Dora was like and guess nobody ever tell them. When she arrive home the baby have bright scarlet cheeks and sores on his face and bottom. But Mad Etta doctored him both inside and out and he is healthy now.

And I never seen anybody as happy as Kingston Oldshoes. He lean down over the bed, talk to Baby Jonah in Cree. Talk to him sometimes like he was a baby, sometimes like he is growed up.

It take a long time for Kingston's bent old hands to change a diaper, but he grin while he doing it, start a smile from

7

way down at his chin work it all the way up to his ears.

"I got nothing else to do with my time," he say. "I'm too old to hunt or dance. But it feel good to know I got to live another fifteen years or so until Jonah be a man."

The Women's Sewing Circle who meet at Blue Quills on Wednesday nights make for Kingston a kind of reverse papoose holder so he can strap the baby to his chest and carry him around. Kingston look kind of funny careful-stepping his way down to the General Store with the baby buttoned under his mackinaw.

"In the summer I put him in a moss bag like a real Indian baby," Kingston say as he plop a diaper in a pail in the corner. Then he point out the window to where diapers be drying, laid flat on the boughs of a spruce tree, look like splashes of snow.

"Washed them myself," and he nod his head toward a big box of Oxydol sit in the corner on a chair with no back.

But the Welfare people keep coming around, looking, ask questions, then going away, like thieves getting ready to do a crime.

Another day Kingston have me and Etta up to his cabin.

"I'm gonna give him a real Indian name," he say. Then Kingston Oldshoes speak a long word over the baby, and him and Etta chant some old songs. "It was my father's name before me—before the Church handed us out white names like they giving us wampum."

In English the name he give the baby is Kills Many Wolverines Man.

"A good name for an Indian boy," say Kingston, and me and Etta are quick to agree.

While we are there the Welfare ladies come by again.

"I think he would be much better off in a home," one say to the other as if we ain't there or don't understand.

"He was born Indian, you not going to swallow him up

8

in your departments. Are you?" says Kingston.

"Look at this," the Welfare lady say, sweep her hand in a half-circle around the cabin, the tiny blue stone on her little finger glint in the light from the coal-oil lamp. "This is not a fit place for a baby," and she move her tiny foot around on the worn green linoleum, grind dirt under it.

I try to imagine what the cabin look like to a white lady, never been no closer to a reserve than the university: all there is is a bed, the kitchen table, a real old wood-stove with a warming-oven and a reservoir for water on the side of it. The bed is covered with what we call Army Blankets, the colour of cow shit.

"There are no sheets," one lady say in a shocked voice, while she poking around the bed. We stay silent. No use to explain you don't need but blankets when you sleep with your clothes on to keep warm.

"A little bit of dirt never hurt anybody very much," says Mad Etta from the back corner of the cabin where she sit on her tree-trunk chair. She is hanging on to the baby and he look tiny as a puppy clutched to Mad Etta's five-flour-sack dress.

"Don't need no stove in a cabin when you got Mad Etta. There is so much of her she make her own heat, you save all kinds of money on wood and coal," is what I'd like to say. But white Welfare ladies ain't ones for joking around so I keep quiet.

Things move fast after that day. Kingston get a big letter with two dollars worth of stamps on it one day, and the next a carload of Welfare people show up on the reserve. Got a man with them, I guess in case of trouble.

They present more papers with red seals on them to Kingston and say they going to take Jonah away to a home in the city for orphan babies.

"I'm too old to fight and too crippled to run," say King-

9

ston as he unbuttons the baby from the nest on his chest.

A Welfare lady wrap Jonah in a white blanket, get into the open door of the long, grey, Government car and drive off.

Next day some of us talk to Ballard Longbow who used to be a big wheel with Indian Affairs and he say he try to get us a meeting in Edmonton with the Welfare peoples at the end of the month.

But it was only about two weeks later that somebody from the Department of the Attorney General sent the telegram to Kingston Oldshoes. Only Mad Etta seem to remember the last time anybody on the reserve got a telegram. It printed up on yellow paper and got STOP written between each sentence make it awful hard to read. CNR guy drive all the way down from Wetaskiwin in a yellow Volkswagen to deliver it. When he find out Kingston live up in the hills he leave it at the General Store.

I promise to take it up to the cabin for I know Kingston need somebody to read the English words to him. I go first to Mad Etta's and after we open it we decide she should go with me. Louis Coyote loaned his truck to somebody else so we have to walk—Mad Etta groan like a bulldozer all the way up the hill.

"We got bad news for you," says Mad Etta, after Kingston answer the door. "Kills Many Wolverines Man is dead," and she wave the yellow telegram.

"They say what killed him was . . ." and she point her beefy big hand at me.

"Something called Sudden Infant Death Syndrome," I say. Kingston's eyes are blank. "Babies die and nobody knows why," I go on quick. Kingston Oldshoes face grow longer and become expressionless as a pancake.

"That's what *they* say," snort Mad Etta. "But *we* know."

It late afternoon and a light rain falls that could turn to

snow at any time. Mad Etta nudge me forward until I'm inside the cabin, then she waddle in. As she pull the door shut, the dimness close on us like a trap, and as the three of us stand there it just get darker and darker.

INDIAN STRUCK

Being smarter than I used to sure ain't as much fun as I thought it would be. Mr. Nichols, my English teacher and counsellor down at the Tech School in Wetaskiwin, and the guy who read my stories, fix up the spellings, put in those commas and stuff, say to me that I got to read four or five books for every story I write. He get me a used set of the *Encyclopedia Britannica*, say I should start to read it from the very front. Also, when important people come to speak at the school he not only make me go to hear them but he invite me off to lunch with them at the Travelodge in Wetaskiwin. So in the last few months I get to meet a psychiatrist, the Minister of Cultural Affairs in the Conservative Government, and this here Professor from the University at Edmonton, Rudy Wiebe, who write about Big Bear and Louis Riel, and I bet read more books than I've ever seen. Mr. Nichols say my sentences getting longer and I don't mess up as often as I used to. But there is some things happen lately that make me wonder if learn all this extra stuff is worth it.

Like last weekend when our baseball team went off to play in a tournament. Louis Coyote's pickup truck was broke down so we got Father Alphonse from the Residential School to go to Buffalo Plumbing Company in Ponoka and get them to loan us a van to make the trip. Man who own Buffalo Plumbing be a good Catholic. We say for Father Alphonse to tell him that the way we say thank you is to write the word "plumbing" on our uniforms, under the name of our team, which be Hobbema Buffalos, so as to make good advertising for him. Our uniforms got the shape of an Indian head drawed on the front and back with red feathers. We is off to a Sports Day at a farm town 50 miles or so southwest, and as far as we know we going to be the only Indian team there.

As we drive along, Gibson Carry-the-kettle plunk some on his guitar and we sing, *Wasn't God Who Made Honky-tonk Angels*, *Sing Me Back Home*, *Branded Man* and lots of other songs we heard from the radio.

In the truck there is me, my friend Frank Fence-post, his brother Charlie, Robert Coyote, Eathen Firstrider, Gibson Carry-the-kettle, Fred Piche, Tommy Halter, Winston Fire-in-the-draw, and a couple of other guys, plus Father Alphonse. Father Alphonse say it is to pray for the baseball team that he goes but we all know that it is to keep an eye on the truck, see we don't race nobody on the highway, and that whoever drives have a driver's licence and don't drink no beer. We got three cases of Lethbridge Pale Ale stashed in among the bags of equipment. We don't want Father Alphonse to know, but guess it ain't much of a secret cause the bottles sure clank a lot when we drive on rough road.

We don't play in no regular league or like that. Tried it one summer but nobody could ever remember when the games was and we was always showing up to play a day early or a day late, so we got dropped out of the league. Couple of times a year there be big Indian pow-wows and sports days where we play in tournaments, or sometimes, like today we go to sports days not too far from Hobbema. We never been known to get past the first round of a tournament.

13

Gibson Carry-the-kettle be a pretty good pitcher; he weigh 250 pounds and can sometimes look mean enough at a batter that they don't hit too often. I play in right field, the place where the other team is least likely to hit the ball. My friend Frank Fence-post is the catcher and he say he get tired every game just from running to the backstop for balls he missed.

Buffalos ain't a very original name for our team either. Some of the Indian teams give themselves real good names like the Frog Lake Massacres, and a reserve town up in Saskatchewan call their team the Wounded Knees. Sometimes while we drive along we make up team names. Frank joke a lot about what the guys from Indian Head, Saskatchewan would call their team.

By the time we get to town the tournament already started, lucky we wasn't supposed to play an early game. We park the van out past centre field and all of us walk around have a quick look at the sports day. We was all gonna bring our girlfriends but Father Alphonse say it ain't legal for so many peoples to ride in one van. I'm not sure if priests know about all the stuff that go on between men and women, if they do they sure turn their eyes away and pretend they don't.

"We figure we could bring as many people as we want, with you along, Father Alphonse," say Frank Fence-post. "You could just pray away the RCMP if they was to decide to hassle us." But Father Alphonse don't change his mind and we leave the girls at home, make sour faces at us as we drive away. I sure wished they could of come along.

The ball field is on the edge of town and just been mowed that morning, smell strong of sweet clover, and some big bumble-bees grumble around wonder what people doing on their field. There is a long, low, community hall, and some little booths made of new lumber and covered with canvas where they sell pop, hot dogs and have a blackjack, an over and under game and a roulette wheel.

We take out some baseballs and start to play catch with each other. Our uniforms ain't exactly uniforms, just sweaters that we pull on over our shirts. We wear jeans for pants and all but Gibson Carry-the-kettle have running-shoes or street shoes. Gibson got real baseball spikes that he say cost $50.

Bunch of kids hang around the van ask us questions, like who we going to play, which one of our guys is the pitcher, where Hobbema is, and why our team is called Buffalos? I wanted to call the team Hobbema Painters, but everybody think I'm silly. Hobbema, no matter how much it sound like it, ain't an Indian word. The town was named for a Dutch guy who paint pictures a long time ago.

There is also a couple of girls hang around, lean on the van, giggle quite a bit, smoke cigarettes and talk loud to each other to make us take some notice of them.

Don't take long before they got three or four guys around them. The girls look alike enough to be sisters but they say they is only cousins. Both be sixteen or so, middle height, got long straight hair, wear T-shirts with pictures of Kiss and David Bowie on them, tight jeans and running-shoes. They ain't much for pretty, got long faces with pimples on their chins. One is called Cindy and one Cathy, I ain't sure which is which. I kind of hope that they will go away.

Gibson start dragging the bags of equipment and beer out of the van.

"Hey partner," he yell at Frank Fence-post, "give me a hand here."

"My union don't allow me to lift nothing heavier than ten pounds, except when I take a leak," say Frank, and he grin steady at them two girls, hitch up his jeans to show them the bulge in the front.

Frank, Eathen, Robert and Gibson make lots of joke with the girls, most of them about sex. The girls don't really seem

15

to catch on but they laugh like they do. They are shrill as magpies and I see one of them got dirty fingernails when she rest her white hand on the black paint of the van.

Funny about girls like that. There always seem to be one or two of them wherever we go. In Calgary one time couple of white girls latch on to me and Frank and we finally have to sneak away from them 'cause they want to come home to Hobbema with us. These white girls sometimes make themselves up to be whiter than they really is by dye their hair yellow or even silver. Cindy and Cathy got pale brown hair, but they wear white lipstick and creamy looking eye-shadow. Girls like these is what we call Indian Struck, and usually, like these two, is kind of ugly. Except one time there was this really pretty girl at the Ponoka Stampede, hang around the corrals and make out with most of the Indian rodeo guys.

I remember a few years ago Alf Blanket is marry one of them Indian Struck girls. Her name was Bonnie and she come from up around the town of Millet. She have bright yellow hair, be a little bit fat, and her front teeth cross over each other. She left Alf after a year or so and I remember him saying a funny thing in the bar of the Alice Hotel one night.

"She left me 'cause I didn't treat her as bad as she thought I should of," and he laugh a kind of sad laugh and shake his head a lot.

Pretty soon Robert Coyote got one of them girls pushed up against the back of the van. They kissing each other like they mean it and he got his hand down inside the front of her jeans. The other girl is hang on to Gibson Carry-the-kettle. Ain't long before Gibson open up the back of the van, spread around the extra sweaters and clothes to make, not so much a bed as a nest, and him and his girl drop right down into it. Robert take his woman up there too and lay her down beside Gibson's woman. I close up the back door of the van 'cause I sure don't want people walking by to see. No matter how free our country supposed to be it still ain't a good idea for Indians to mess with white girls in a white town. Frank suggest we should have a sign on the van like one we seen on a van on a used-car lot in Wetaskiwin say, "If this van is rockin' don't bother knockin'."

It sure lucky that Father Alphonse gone off, I guess to look for other priests to talk to. Charlie Fence-post and Fred Piche take a turn with them girls after Robert and Gibson is finished, and most of the other guys was waiting to except we get the call to play ball on the field.

We paired up against a team from Drayton Valley, call themselves the Dodgers. They got regular uniforms, spiked shoes, a couple of coaches and a whole bunch of extra players.

Today, Gibson Carry-the-kettle pitch only in the general direction of the plate. By the third inning Frank he just walk to the backstop after missed balls, let the base runners go wherever they like. Drayton Valley is already ahead 17–1, but we is supposed to play five innings no matter how hard we losing. When Gibson do let them hit the ball one of us miss it. I run in about five steps on a fly ball before I realize that it going about ten steps over my head.

We sure glad when the fifth inning is over and it only 28–1. We shake hands with the Dodgers and tell them, good game.

"You guys are lucky we was playing good," say Frank, "or you would of really beat us. If we wasn't *on* it could of taken another couple of hours to get in five innings."

The Dodgers suggest we should all go up to the community hall where they is serving up roast-chicken dinners for $2, cooked up by the ladies of the local church.

Some of us start off for the hall and some head back for the van with them Indian Struck girls. The girls been sit close to our bench during the game and one even come right over and do some kissing with Frank Fence-post between innings, which draw some dirty looks from some of the crowd.

The community hall was built about 50 years ago or so, have just rough boards for a floor. We come up to it from the back and can see through the open doors that there be three or four big black stoves in the back where the women is busy cook up dinners. There is wooden tables fill up the rest of the hall, with benches down each side and it be over half full with people eating their dinners.

We pay our $2 and go get our plate of food. Boy, it sure smell good in there. We get a plate full of chicken dinner, a piece of pie and cup of coffee, then we go to find us a place to sit on one of the benches. Just as we gonna sit down a skinny young guy in a blue jacket, got oily hair and eyes kind of bulge out of his face, tap Winston Fire-in-the-draw on the arm and ask if he wouldn't rather eat outside.

Winston is about to say okay and start for the door, when one of the Dodgers, a guy built wide, and low to the ground like a jeep, step up to this kid and look right into his chest.

"You saying these guys can't eat in here because they're Indians?" he growl in a deep voice.

The kid's eyes pop out a little more than usual. "It wasn't my idea," he say. "The Mayor told me to say it." And he slink away real fast, come back with a man we guess is the Mayor. He is about 60 wear baggy brown pants and a blue suit jacket look about as old as he is. He have a long, thin face come to a point at the chin. His cheeks be blue as saw-blades even though they been shaved.

"You got something against Indians?" the Dodger say to him. The Mayor he look mean at him but meaner at me and Winston, and he stay quiet a long time, like he figuring if it going to be worth the trouble to explain why Indians shouldn't be allowed to eat with white people.

"That kid's not very smart," he say through his yellow teeth, "he must have misunderstood. I said to keep drunks out, both Indian and white," and he smile a bit by twitch one corner of his mouth up higher than the rest of his face.

What I recognize and what scare my heart until it beat up in my chest like somebody flick a finger on a balloon, is the face of the Mayor and the faces of them girls back in the truck: they is got to be relatives of some kind. I just figure that if a guy like him ever knew what was happening that there be RCMP and farmers with guns all over the place in no time. Small town like this, them girls bound to be somebody's sisters or daughters. Indian guys could get in a lot of trouble—girls like that could easy yell "rape" and who you think gonna get believed, the white girls or a truckload of Indians?

By the time I get back to the van, I take as long as I can lose a dollar on the over and under game on the way, guess I be the only one who ain't had a turn with those girls. Frank Fence-post meet me grinning big through the hole in his face where he had some teeth knocked out in a fight in the Alice Hotel Bar. He tell me about how he been with each one of them in about as many ways as a man and woman can get together, grin some more and I can see it make him feel really big to tell me this.

Gibson Carry-the-kettle slap his hand on the back door of the van, yell for Eathen and whoever else is in there to hurry up 'cause I'm there waiting.

I sort of look up at the sky to show that the sun is going down. "Wouldn't want to get caught by Father Alphonse," I say and smile like I sad. "I just skip it this time," even though I say that my voice don't sound like I mean it.

"Hey partner," says Frank, "what's the matter with you? We got a truck full of chicken dinner here, a little white meat be soft and tender and warm and taste good," and he slap me on the back. Just then Eathen climb out of the van doing up his jeans and nod for me to climb in. The warm air follow him out, smell of beer and woman and plumbing tools.

"So when are you and Sadie getting married?" one of the guys say. Sadie One-wound is my girlfriend. Then all the guys give me a hard time.

"Hey, Frank," one of the girls call out. "Come here for a minute, I want to see you."

"I know what she wants to see," says Frank as he smile big and climb up into the van. And I remember how the last time we met up with an Indian Struck girl I was just like Frank and come away feeling happy and strong. Something like that always been fun 'cause it was dangerous, and it fun to get to mess with a white girl too. Most white girls don't have nothing to do with us Indians. A bunch of us quite often sit in the booth in the window of the Gold Nugget Café in Wetaskiwin, watch white girls walk by and dream about what it be like to go to bed with them.

I don't argue with the guys and pretty soon they leave me alone. I let them believe it because of my girlfriend Sadie that I don't take my turn.

It was just a couple of weeks ago that I asked Mr. Nichols about how come 99% of white girls turn up their noses and don't want nothing to do with us Indians but then that other 1% be what we call Indian Struck.

"You probably aren't going to like what I tell you, Silas," Mr. Nichols he say to me. Then he go on to say that it ain't because we're such great studs and all that these girls want to have sex with us. He say that somewhere along the line them Indian Struck girls been raised up so they don't like themselves at all.

"They have no self-esteem," be how Mr. Nichols put it.

In their minds these girls don't like themselves, so they don't like their bodies either. They figure, what is the worst-thing I can do to my body, and the answer they think of is to let it be used by men that nobody else think much of, like Indians.

Knowing all that kind of take the fun out of partying with Indian Struck girls. I let the guys kid me some more on the way home. I know some of them sure to tell Sadie and that going to put me in good with her. I could tell them what I know, but if Frank and Robert and the other guys want to think that it is because they walk around with a bulge in their jeans that these girls come after them, then why should I tell them different? They'd figure I was making it up anyway, or that I was showing off 'cause I read books and had some of my stories printed up.

THE SISTERS

On this site will be built The Three Seeds of the Spirit, Predestinarian, Bittern Lake Baptist Church. That's what the sign say beside the road just a half-mile or so from Bittern Lake. I have to write down careful the big word in the middle. I didn't know what it meant then and I still don't.

The reason me and Frank Fence-post pulled over Louis Coyote's pickup truck was that there be two white ladies standing by the sign waving their hands at us.

"Oh my goodness," say one of them, "you must be Indians."

"Either that or buffalo," says Frank.

"Oh, no," say the smallest lady. "Buffalo are much larger." Then she clap her little hand over her mouth like she say something bad. "You were teasing us," she say and smile, and her face look like it peeking out of a little white cloud.

"We don't tease white ladies," say Frank. "My friend here be 50% buffalo."

In a way that is true. My mother's name was Suzie Buffalo before she married up to Paul Ermineskin.

"What are your names?" the tallest white lady say.

"I'm Silas Ermineskin," I say, "and this is . . ." but before I can say Frank Fence-post, Frank say, "Chief Dan George. Would you like me to sign my name for you?" Frank would sure be in trouble if they did 'cause at the best of times he is only able to write part of his name.

That sign is sitting off the edge of the highway on land that slope down to Bittern Lake, which is a pretty cold place. The wind whip across the bluey ice of the lake in winter make wolf-howl sounds, and in summer the lake hardly ever get warm enough to swim in.

The name Chief Dan George usually mean something to people. Him being a movie star make him about the only Indian name most people know besides Tonto and Geronimo. But these little ladies don't smile or nothing, they just shake our hands very serious like. The littlest one got skin as pink as the wild roses that bloom in the ditch, and fluffy white hair. She is lucky to be five feet tall and a sack of flour outweigh her by ten pounds.

"His name is really Frank Fence-post," I say. "Chief Dan George just be his name when he's on television."

"Fence is a strange first name, don't you think, Martha?" the tiny one say to the tall one, just as if we weren't there at all.

"Not any stranger than Ermine," the tall one answer back. She got a brown handkerchief tied over her head, be scrawny as a starved dog and have little brown eyes way down deep in her face.

I explain real careful that our names are Frank and Silas, not Fence and Ermine, and how us Indians have two or more part names, like Fire-in-the-draw, Carry-the-kettle, One-wound and a lot of others.

"We're going to build a church," say Lucy, the one with white hair.

"In memory of our brother," say Martha.

"Wasn't this Billygoat Barnes' land?" ask Frank. I been thinking the same thing and been peeking down the hill trying to see if his cabin was down there somewhere.

23

"Our brother was Sebastian Barnes," say Martha.

"We are living in his home," say Lucy.

These little ladies sure have a funny accent of some kind. Billygoat Barnes was from Tennessee in the United States, and I guess these sisters of his must be from there too.

Billygoat Barnes was a funny little man, must of been 80 years old when he died. He had an acre or two of land run from the lake to the highway, and a cabin he built mostly of slabs and tin cans. He had whiskers all around his face, sticking straight out like a toilet brush, and he was called Billygoat on account of the way he smelled. He always had an old felt hat pulled down over his ears. Somewhere back on his land he had a still and sold home-brew to anybody who had money. Not the kind of guy I would think of building a church for.

"Who's gonna build this here church for you?" ask Frank.

"Why Fence," says Miss Lucy, "we were hoping you would."

"We just stop our truck 'cause you look like you were in trouble," we say.

"And so we were. By the way, have you young men been born again?"

"Once was enough for me," say Frank.

"I seen a story on the TV," I say, "about a guy who said he'd been born quite a few times. Said he was a Japanese wrestler one time, and a slave in Africa another. . . ."

"Are you Christians?" say Miss Martha.

"We're Catholic, I guess," I tell her. Most everybody on the reserve been signed up by the Catholic church at one time or another. We also know what it is these ladies is talking about, we got Pentecostal ministers, Four-Square ministers and Beulah Tabernacle ministers come around the reserve try to convert us to their ways. We tease them along too. One time the Beulah Tabernacle man bought about ten of us lunch at the Woolworth's store in Wetaskiwin. Another time, two Jehovah's Witness ladies, look mean as dried apples, pay for some of us to go bowling 'cause we promise sure to come to their church on Sunday.

"Our first converts," say Miss Lucy.

"Oh, Sister, I'm so happy," say Miss Martha.

"Just a minute," I say. "You going too quick for us. We help you some way if you in trouble. . . ."

"Oh Ermine, would you? We need help to clean out Sebastian's cabin."

Them white ladies sure ain't lazy. They work right beside us, lift up boxes twice as big as themselves. Billygoat Barnes must of been part packrat 'cause he got stuff in his cabin that ain't been used for 50 years. The place has boxes full of broke harness, car parts, bottles and his bedroom be full with most of a threshing machine.

After we finish, Miss Lucy dig around in the big black bag she carry on her arm. "I can only find one dime," she say to Miss Martha.

Miss Martha dig down in her purse, come up with a coin and they each give us a shiny silver dime.

"Oh boy," say Frank, "now I be able to afford a college education, not have to work like this anymore."

I poke his arm to be quiet 'cause I think these ladies be serious about what they doing. I take the dimes and press them back in Miss Lucy's hands. "What we'd really like is some beads or bright coloured buttons," I say as serious as I know how. They both start digging in their purses again. "But you don't have to pay us today, some other time will do."

"Fence and Ermine," Miss Lucy say, her face all pink as a real delicate sunrise, "we want to thank you for your help. You may be pagans but we want you to know that we think there is hope for you, and we'd like you to come back the same time tomorrow."

Then they give us each a copy of *The Sword of the Lord*, a little newspaper full of religious writing, and say God Bless us a few times. I read a little bit of that paper and it seem funny to me that them people don't like nobody that don't believe just as they do. Everybody else, they say, is going for sure to hell. I always heard religious people was supposed to tolerate them who think different, but then none that I've met ever seem to.

We don't go back the next day or the day after for that matter. The third afternoon a bunch of us is down at the pool-hall at Hobbema when Robert Coyote come in, say, "Couple of white women outside looking for some God-fearing Indians named Fence and Ermine. Anybody here know a couple of God-fearing Indians like that?" Everybody have a good laugh at us, especially Robert who is about the toughest dude around the reserve.

Frank and me, we go outside real slow and our girlfriends go with us. Sadie One-wound is mine. Connie Bigcharles is his.

Miss Lucy and Miss Martha look us up and down with a steady brown stare. Nobody say anything and the little ladies smile at us kind of shy.

"Well, we was gonna come back," say Frank. "In a day or two."

"How'd you ladies get down here?" I ask.

"Sister and I just walked over to the main highway and stuck out our thumbs," say Sister Lucy.

"And that nice young man picked us up and brought us right here," say Sister Martha, wave her hand toward the pool-hall to show that it was Robert who picked them up. I wonder how nice they'd think Robert was if they knew how many times he been in jail.

We introduce our girlfriends to them.

"Our little flock grows, Sister," says Miss Lucy.

Sadie kind of get behind me. She is real shy with white people, but nobody scares Connie very much. Connie got lots of green eye-makeup all around her big brown eyes. She wearing tight jeans, cowboy boots and an open denim vest over a pink blouse that have no bra under it. Connie's breasts is shaped like wasps' nests and about the same size. The church ladies' eyes get almost as big as Connie's when they look at her.

"What is it you'd like from us today?" I ask.

"Why we need help to dig a basement for the church. We've been to Wetaskiwin and have our permit to dig it and everything," say the sisters, smiling real nice at us.

"How come you old ladies want to build a church anyway?" say Connie.

I give her a sharp look but she just shrug her shoulders. When Connie want to know something she don't see no harm in asking.

"We want to create a haven for poor underprivileged people like yourselves. Church is the only place you can go with tears in your eyes and not have anyone ask why it is you're crying," say Miss Lucy in a real serious voice. Her and Miss Martha are both smile real sweet at us. We think on what she say for a minute.

"What about at a funeral home?" I say.

"Or an onion-eating contest?" says Frank.

"Or a sad movie?" say Connie.

"Or if you was to choke on your beer?" yell Frank, jumping up and down some.

The little ladies stay calm until we finally run out of ideas.

"Primitive, Sister, very primitive," sniff Sister Martha.

"We also want the church to be a suitable monument for our dear brother," say Sister Lucy.

"I guess if anybody need a church built for him it would

be Billygoat Barnes," I say.

"You'll come with us then?" say Sister Martha.

"I suppose," we say.

"One thing bother me though," I say. "Could the reason that you come around trying to get Indians to work for you for nothing be that you got no money to pay anybody with?"

"We own the land," say Lucy.

"We have our pensions," say Miss Martha.

"But you got no money?"

"The Lord will provide," they say together.

"Just like he is providing us?" say Frank.

"Exactly," they say to us, and then they say "Hallelujah" a couple of times to each other.

It hard to make a good argument against tough little ladies like that. We go borrow Louis Coyote's truck, load them up and head off for Bittern Lake.

They got stakes and strings laid out and they show us where we supposed to dig the basement and hand us each a shiny new shovel. After an hour or so we get pretty tired. By that time we only got a hole big enough for a shallow grave dug. That ground be hard and have more rocks than I ever care to see.

"You can just bury me," say Frank flopping down on his back in the cool ground like he was to make a snow angel. "I done me enough church digging for one day." I agree with him. "Why don't we go down to Roychuck's Equipment and see if we can steal us a bulldozer?" say Frank. "It take us a year, full time, to dig a hole as big as they want."

We decide to go for a walk by the lake. The church ladies got our girlfriends down at the cabin washing the windows and the floor and shine things up.

"Does your mother know you smoke?" Sister Lucy is saying to Connie Bigcharles as we come down the hill.

"She learned from me," says Connie, roll her eyes and

28

blow some smoke at the sky.

We take the girls and walk on down by the lake. The ladies ask a lot of questions about how the basement is coming but we don't answer them.

"How are we gonna get these ladies uninterested in build a church?" I ask.

"They think they own us," says Connie.

"We could all go up to Edmonton until fall," says Frank. "They never be able to find us there."

"They say we gonna be in their choir," say Sadie in a real small voice. "Silas, I'm scared to sing."

Frank is running ahead along what little beach there is. It is all covered with stones the colour of seagulls. All of a sudden, like dropping a rock in a river, Frank disappear right into the ground.

When we look down in the hole there is Frank sit on the floor at the bottom all covered in sand and dirt.

"I must of missed the stairs," he say to us and shake some of the dirt out of his hair.

The three of us stand around the hole, lean forward from the neck to look down at Frank.

"There's a whole big cave down here," he say, "look like it run way up under the hill. Come on down and we go have a look at it."

Connie and me jump down, bring with us a shower of sand and dirt that get in my hair and tickle on the back of my neck like maybe ants walk there.

Our eyes get used to the dark pretty quick. We can see way off a little touch of light like a yellow stick been poked into the dark.

In 50 feet or so the tunnel widen out on one side to make a room and boy there is so much equipment there that it look like the science laboratory down to the Tech School. There is copper pipe coiled around like a whole lot of frozen

29

snakes, glass jars, barrels, measuring cups, and stacked around the walls is sacks of malt and grain and sugar, all the stuff you ever need to make enough home-brew to fill up Bittern Lake if it was ever to run dry.

"Hey, we is rich Indians," says Frank. "We make up enough home-brew that we buy a car when we sell it all," and Frank and Connie dance around the dark little room.

"Either of you know how to work a still?" I ask.

"No," they say, "but it can't be too hard. You just mix grain, malt and sugar until it bubble up and smell bad. Then you bottle it and sell it."

"My guess be that there is more to it than that," I say. "We should think on it for a while. We probably have to give out a share to somebody who know about stills."

That somebody would be Carl Sorenson from Wetaskiwin. Carl run Carl's Used Furniture and Secondhand Store from his house by the UGG elevator across from the Canadian Legion. The front yard of his house be full of rusty ploughs, broke stoves, car wheels with grass grown up through them, and maybe 50 other kinds of junk. Inside it be just as crowded as the yard. The front window be full of tall geraniums, glass ornaments and dead flies. The window ain't been washed I bet for twenty years.

Carl don't sell much used stuff but everybody know that he do an awful good trade in home-brew at night after the bars close and on Sundays with both white people and Indians. All you got to have to do business with Carl is money.

He is a Swedish man who had a half Indian mother, stand real tall, but from his waist up he be shaped like a triangle with a big gut drop over his belt that he got probably from sample too much of his own product. He ain't too crazy about having Indians around who aren't buying anything and it take us quite a while to talk him into coming out to look at what we found.

"After Billygoat died I snooped all around his place trying to find his still," say Carl.

"You just didn't step in the right place," says Frank and get a funny look from Carl for saying it.

We make sure he bring along some good flashlights. The entrance to the tunnel was at the top of the hill not 50 feet from where we building the church. There be a lift-up door all covered over by raspberry canes. We all scratch ourselves some getting in. On the way to the still we find something we missed the first time: off to one side in a little rocky room is what must be a thousand bottles and jugs of home-brew, enough to fill up a couple of Alberta Government Liquor Stores. We stop and take a sample drink. Carl smack his lips and say how good it is and so do we, even though Frank choke some while he saying it. Then Carl size up the brewing equipment.

"Best set-up I ever seen," says Carl.

"We thought you'd like it," we say. We sure wish we'd found all those bottles before we brought him in on it.

"Is it for sale, or what?"

"Rent."

"Rent?"

"Half of what you take in you keep," we say. "The rest go half for us and half for the church ladies. Only for the ladies you buy lumber and nails and pay for men to work on the church. They just gonna think you is the most generous man in the county."

"How do you know you can trust me?" says Carl.

"We know you couldn't take a blood test without cheating," we tell him. "That's why you be easy to deal with. If you don't play fair we tell the RCMP where to find the still and you be out of business and into jail."

"You'd do that to a brother?" say Carl. He only call us

brother when he want something. The rest of the time we be wagonburners.

"Wouldn't be much of a brother would cheat his friends," we say. Then we all shake hands and crack one of Billygoat Barnes' bottles of raisin wine to celebrate the deal. We sure surprised it go so easy. Carl could of got us to take maybe $50 each, and we'd never tell the RCMP the right time of day, even on a white man.

We get us a big rush of money at first as Carl come down every night for a load of home-brew and sell off the stock what Billygoat had built up. In the day he come around with material he donate to the church.

"That nice Mr. Sorenson brought us some plumbing pipe today and tomorrow he's going to bring a plumber," say Sister Lucy to me one afternoon. "Now who can say the Lord doesn't provide? You didn't think we could do it, did you, Ermine?"

"No ma'am, I didn't," I say. That church is filling out nice and some other people have been asking around about maybe joining when it is finished. There be a lot of religious people around Camrose and Wetaskiwin and I guess some of them be ready for a change.

After the foundation been poured and some walls in place on three sides, the open studs looking like the ribs of some big dead animal, the sisters invite down from Camrose the Minister Man from the Fundamental Baptist Church of the Fourth Dimension, a Pastor Orkin.

This here Fundamental Church don't have many members and they don't have a church. They hold their services in the Sons of Sweden Community Hall about half-way between Camrose and Bittern Lake, and in the summer spend a lot of time dunk each other in lakes, creeks and when nothing else available, pails full of water. Sister Lucy figures that when the church is built it would be nice if they was to "amalgamate" with each other, and she tell all this to Pastor Orkin, as they walk around make hollow sounds with their feet on the rough flooring.

Pastor Orkin is young for a minister, like about 35, got red cheeks and yellow hair been cut by a barber and sprayed full of stuff to make it lie down. His hands is soft and red like his face and he clasp them in front of his belly and make motions like he got a tennis ball that he rubbing around.

Him and the little ladies get along good until they tell him about how they "converted" us heathen Indians into their church and how happy we all going to be together.

When he hear that Pastor Orkin's eyes get big and his nose flare out like a horse that smell a thunderstorm coming.

"Indians can't belong to our church," he say.

"For heaven's sake, why not?" say the sisters.

"Their skin, Sisters, their skin. The good Lord punished them by not making them white. Our church must be kept pure. . . ."

"Hey, that's okay with us," we say. "We just sort of resign, okay? Don't want to cause nobody no trouble." Never thought we'd be arguing with a people who got mean ideas like that, but it look like a good way for us to get out of going to that church. Sister Martha already got me lined up to drive the school bus, if and when they get a school bus.

"But they're our first converts," say the Sisters, and Sister Lucy has took ahold of Connie's hand and stand close beside her.

"They are inferior in other ways too," say Pastor Orkin. "Their intelligence is lower, their heads are harder, they have criminal tendencies and are morally degenerate. . . ."

"You mean we is all those bad things just because of our skin colour?"

That minister's eyes run fast from side to side when he speak.

"God punished you for your sins in another life by giving you dark skin in this one."

"What do you figure is darker than black?" say Frank. "That's what colour I coming back next time."

"Suppose that mean we can't go to your heaven either?" I say.

"That is correct," say Pastor Orkin, his hands clasped together like big pink pork chops.

"You hear that, Frank?" I say. "We never gonna get ourselves to heaven. We don't get to live with the Pastor there after we die."

"Well, Silas, we don't let him come to our heaven either. My happy hunting ground have lots of blond white girls in a line-up waiting to get at my body."

"And Alberta Government Liquor Stores with no clerks . . . we just go right in and help ourselves . . ." I say.

"And hotels that don't charge for rooms . . ."

". . . and don't care if you bring in some friends for a party . . ."

". . . and taxi drivers who don't take you the long way . . . or rip you off . . ."

". . . and new cars that don't need drivers' licences or insurance or registration stuff to drive . . ." says Frank.

"And free cowboy boots," says Connie.

"And trail bikes . . ."

"And warm houses . . ."

"And where everybody have their own tape-deck and guitar . . ."

". . . and free eye-shadow and lipstick . . ."

". . . and red dresses," say Sadie, open her mouth for the first time, as all four of us join hands and dance in a loud circle on the first layer of floor.

"I've heard quite enough," say Pastor Orkin. "The white race is superior in all ways to the coloured races."

"Do you know how to speak Cree?" say Frank to the pastor.

"Of course not," he say back, like it is a silly question.

"Then how's it feel to be dumber than an Indian?" say Frank, and the four of us jump up and down some more.

Then something happen that really surprise us. Sister Lucy and Sister Martha come over and stand beside us.

"I'm afraid our church will just have to get along as best we can," Sister Lucy say to the pastor while Sister Martha move her lips along with her. Sister Lucy pick up one of my big brown hands in her tiny white one. "Our friends are part of our flock...."

"We's the whole damn thing," says Frank, and grin big while both Connie and me shush him.

"... and if you won't allow them to join then we'll have to get along without you."

Pastor Orkin weasel around for a little while 'cause he can see his free church building floating off from him. He quote some Bible to show he is right and when that don't work he tell the sisters that they going to hell right along with us, but the little sisters just stand solid beside us and finally Pastor Orkin get in his car.

"During the week I work in the Accounts Payable Department at the John Deere plant. You can find me there if you come to your senses," he say and slam his car door.

We is in kind of a bad spot, us Indians. These little white ladies stuck out their necks for us and now even Frank feel a little guilty when he look at them 'cause we taking some of their money and we know the money that building their church come from a place they sure wouldn't like if they knew.

I remember one day we bring with us a few beers roll

around in a washtub in the back of the pickup and Sister Martha give us a lecture about how bad beer is for us and then she sit down on the edge of the foundation and sing what she call "temperance songs," all about how awful booze is. The songs is about little kids trying to drag their daddies out of saloons and stuff like that. I agree with her that beer cause most of the trouble for us Indians, but singing songs about it don't help much that I can see.

We've told Carl Sorenson to save up our money until we got a thousand dollars and then we figure to go buy ourselves a car. We only make one mistake and that is telling Carl about how the sisters turn away Pastor Orkin because of us Indians.

"You really like those white ladies?" he say to us, and we all smile and agree we do. Carl he smile with us but his smile is like a fox and I wonder at the time what is turning in his head.

We find out a couple of days later when we go by to see how the church is coming.

Sister Martha come out to meet us.

"Why Ermine and Fence," she say, "we are surprised you would do such a thing to us."

"Huh," we say, but I get a feeling like the bottom falling out of my stomach.

"That nice Mr. Sorenson came around this morning and said how you had been selling him some of Sebastian's farm implements and materials. He said he felt so badly about what you were doing that he donated all his profits back to the church in the form of lumber and supplies and by hiring tradesmen." She stop then and look at us like maybe she want us to defend ourselves. I nod my head to Frank and he run off quick to see what Carl been up to, though we both know he probably already cleared out with everything that have any value.

36

Sister Lucy has come along by now and she look disappointed at me too. "And we had such wonderful news," she say. "When we went down into the little root-cellar under the house we found some jam tins full of money. Sebastian must have saved it when he sold his crops. There's more money than we'll ever need to finish the church. I wonder what Sebastian raised to make so much money from such a small farm?"

"Seagulls," I tell her.

"Seagulls?" she say. "I don't see any around here. Why we're thousands of miles from an ocean."

"Old Billygoat caught them all," I say. "Used to be Bittern Lake was covered in seagulls. He shipped off a truckload every week for years. There used to be a seagull packing plant in Edmonton, but it closed down after your brother went out of business."

Both sisters look some relieved. It seem to me that there ain't nothing that little old white ladies won't believe.

Frank come running back. "Everything's gone," he say. "Ain't nothing left but the cave and the beach."

"That nice Mr. Sorenson told us that he was supposed to hold your ill-gotten gains for you, but he said that being a good Christian he just couldn't bring himself to do it so he donated all you had coming to the church," and Sister Martha looked awful pleased with herself.

"How much?" I say.

"A hundred dollars. He's such a nice honest man, why he even carried off a whole truckload of junk, pipes and jars and goodness knows what, and he did it for nothing too, just out of his Christian charity."

I'm figuring in my head that Carl must of owed us near to a thousand dollars, but now he have that still stuff hid off in the bush where it take us a year to find it if we was to look.

Me and Frank look at each other, make sad faces and

shrug our shoulders. "Pastor Orkin was right about us Indians," I say. "We is bad buggers, excuse the language."

As we walk off toward the truck the sisters is working a paintbrush on the outside of a wall and singing in their squeaky old voices, sound like cartoons on the television:

We never eat fruitcake
Because it has rum
And one little bite
Turns a man to a bum
O can you imagine
A sadder disgrace
Than a bum in the gutter
With crumbs on his face.

JOKEMAKER

"Trusting the government is like asking Colonel Sanders to babysit your chickens," say Ballard Longbow, and about a hundred or so people in Blue Quills Hall laugh, clap their hands and cheer some.

Ballard is President of the Alberta Native Brotherhood, and tonight is one of those meetings where the big wheels from Department of Indian Affairs come around. They do that maybe twice a year, listen for an hour or two then tell us how good we really got it, and take their airplanes back to Ottawa for another six months.

Up on the stage is Ballard, Chief Tom Crow-eye, and six guys from Indian Affairs. All but one of the white men got big bellies, pink cheeks and suits that shine like moonlight on water. Most of them speak with French accents. The different one is a Mr. Wellsley. He is slim, half-way bald; his hair stop growing just about on a line with his ears. He wears a black suit and though he sit with his hands tight in his lap, his eyes tour around the hall like they was blue ballbearings.

Ballard gets good laughs from everybody by making a lot of fun on Indian Affairs, the Prime Minister, the Premier of Alberta, but always he save his best shot for Chief Tom Crow-eye, who besides be our chief here on the Ermineskin

Reserve is the MLA for Wetaskiwin in Premier Lougheed's government.

"I hear Chief Tom was the only Indian at a big government cocktail party. A cocktail party, that's where they take the bottle out of the brown bag before they drink it," and he stick the needle in Chief Tom about ten more times. Most of his jokes are more mean than funny but then most jokes are.

"Did you hear about the day Chief Tom locked his keys in his car? Three of his staff had to sit in the car for four hours while he went to get help."

Chief Tom and the Indian Affairs people make smiles with their teeth but not with their eyes.

Ballard Longbow always been able to mix up funny and serious business. He is a good jokemaker. He tell Peigan jokes. Peigans is some Indians who live way off in the south end of the province. "You hear about the four Peigans froze to death last winter? They went to see a drive-in movie called *Closed for the Season*."

White peoples all the time tell me about how much of a sense of humour us Indians got. I ask Ballard about that one time. "When we're down as low as we are on the totem pole then the only thing there is to do is laugh. You got to laugh just to survive."

One thing I've never quite understood is why white men don't tell jokes about Indians. White men here in Alberta tell mostly Ukrainian jokes. I asked Mr. Nichols, my English teacher and counsellor down to the Wetaskiwin Tech School, about it once.

He say it have something to do with what he call claim to territory. The last group to get to a place is the ones get jokes told about them. "The Ukrainians were the last big minority to come to the prairies, people didn't understand their customs or language so they assumed that they were dumb,"

Mr. Nichols say.

Nowadays people make as many jokes on Pakistanis as Ukrainians, but they hardly ever tell Indian jokes, even though we be the poorest, least educated minority around. Maybe it *is* because we was here first. No matter who telling, the one thing I notice is that the joke is always on somebody else.

Indians tell Indian jokes. Always it is on a tribe we hardly know of except by name. We take Ukrainian jokes and make them into Peigan jokes, or Sarcee jokes and we suppose *they* probably make Cree jokes.

"You hear about the Peigan dog who got a foot caught in a leg-hold trap? He chew off three of his feet but the fourth one was still caught in the trap."

Ballard Longbow is short and stocky. He wear a suede suit, a bright red tie and polished shoes. He got a round face, full lips and wear big, black-rimmed glasses make him look serious even when he is smiling. He be about 30 but can look at you innocent as a child of ten, or talk wise as an old chief.

"We are not children," Ballard say. "We are tired of being treated like children. We are tired of living in isolation. We must rip open the buckskin curtain and make use of the resources available to us to make our lives richer, but at the same time remaining Indians who cherish the past."

This get a big round of applause, even from the people on stage. Guess Ballard figure he been serious long enough so he launch into another story.

"Years ago when I lived on the reserve full-time, we was having a Liar's Contest right here at Blue Quills Hall. We all threw some money in the pot and there was a $50 prize. It was a cold night in the winter and the furnace was smoking a little.

"There was some pretty good lies being told: Rider Stonechild was last and he was in the middle of telling the story of how Augustus Cote turned up at the Catholic Church leading a moose and asked Father Alphonse to marry them, when a white man, wear a suit and hat, stumble in the back door, let in a cloud of steam and snow with him.

"Rider Stonechild stop his story. 'What do you want?' he say to the white man.

" 'I'm from the Government and I want to help you,' the man say.

"Well, we declare the contest over and present that white man with the $50 prize money."

Ballard always spend a lot of time talking about how Indians got to be allowed to manage their own money. "Any time there is a problem, government throw a couple of million dollars at it and hope that it go away. Then they send out a couple of guys from Ottawa who never spent nothing bigger than their pay cheques to manage the money, and we get treated like little kids with rich parents who are afraid money will spoil them, so they give it out a nickel at a time. They are called consultants. A consultant is a high-priced expert who borrow your watch to tell you what time it is, or he is a man who describe 137 ways of making love but then tell you he don't know any women.

"There ain't never been," Ballard go on, "a government employee who will help you do anything—but every one of them will try to keep you from doing something."

The cheering almost shake old Blue Quills Hall off its foundation. Ballard close up by telling some more Peigan jokes.

"These are really white-people jokes," Ballard say, "but if I told them that way white people would get insulted and we wouldn't want that, would we?

"Did you hear about the Peigan who lost $40 on the Grey Cup game? Twenty dollars on the game and twenty dollars on the television replay.

"You hear about the Peigan rapist? Police caught him and put him in a line-up. When the victim walked in, he pointed at her and said, 'That's her!'

"Or how about the Peigan who went ice-fishing. He caught 2000 pounds."

It is my job to clean up Blue Quills Hall after meetings like this, so I am digging in the closet in the washroom for a pail and mop when two of the Indian Affairs men come in to use the bathroom. They don't see me.

"He's dangerous," one of them say.

"Only as long as he's credible," and I recognize it as the voice of the skinny, half-bald man, and can picture his eyes sliding all around in his face like pucks on ice.

"What do you recommend?" say the first voice. "He can cause us a lot of trouble. He has that ability to rouse people."

"I'll take care of it," says Half-bald, "and he'll go out with a whimper instead of a bang. We'll open up his buckskin curtain and invite him inside. We'll kill him with power . . ." and he stop real sudden because somebody else come into the washroom. Sure wish they hadn't 'cause I would of liked to have heard more.

Guess that when Ottawa is up to no good they can move as fast as anyone else, 'cause it is only a month or so later that the big announcement come: Ballard Longbow has been appointed Director General of Indian Affairs in Alberta. He be boss of all the Indian Chiefs and all the Indian Agents and Department of Indian Affairs people for the whole province. He get his picture on the front page of the Edmonton *Journal*, the Calgary *Herald* and the Wetaskiwin *Times*. He is the first Indian ever to get such an important job and they say he make $37,500 a year.

The night we hear about it we all have us a party at Rufus and Winnie Bear's place. "Things gonna be different for us

43

Indians now," we say, though none of us are quite sure how.

"There be more jobs, maybe," somebody say.

"And better schools."

"And lots more money."

"Humff!" Mad Etta snort, sound like the southbound CPR freight when it just start up.

"Ballard Longbow would of starved to death in the old days. He see a herd of buffalo he ride full-blast into the middle of them yelling and whooping like he going to kill them all, instead of riding around the outside of the herd picking them off one at a time."

"So what?" we say at her.

"Even hunting buffalo you got to be patient—deal with something big as government you got to move so slow you always seem to be standing still. I don't think Ballard can do that so he going to be in for a lot of trouble."

We a little bit sorry that Ballard have a white man first name. Some say he got it because there was an Indian Agent named Mr. Ballard here on the reserve about the time he was born, others say he was named for a can of Dr. Ballard's dog food. We say if he had an Indian name it would be Jokemaker, because of all the good stories he tells.

It is a nice feeling to have somebody you know become famous. We are pretty sure that Ballard is going to stay an Indian and not try to turn into a white man like Chief Tom. I worry about what those men talked about in the washroom but I never mention it to Ballard because I wouldn't know how to bring it up. First time we go up to Edmonton to where Ballard got his office we is pretty shy, but when Ballard finds out we're there he invite us right in. We claim to come to ask about a wheelchair been ordered more than a year ago for old Gatien Crier, but really we just want to see how Ballard is doing.

"You look just the same as you do on TV," my friend

44

Frank Fence-post say to him.

"Yeah, those cameras don't really steal your soul like we been told," Ballard says, and we all have a good laugh with him.

He got an office big as a lawyer's with carpet and walls full of books. He also have a white secretary and a whole lot of phones. On the wall of his office he have a painting by Allen Sapp, the Cree Indian artist, that he say cost $4500. When we finally tell him about the wheelchair he just pick up his phone and tell his secretary, "Get me the International Hospital Equipment Company," then when she buzz him back he say to that company, "I want a wheelchair delivered to Hobbema first thing tomorrow." I guess they try to give him some static because he really light into them. "How much business do you figure you get from Indian Affairs?" he ask, but don't wait for an answer. "Well if you ever want any more that chair better be at Hobbema by noon." And he hang up the phone and smile. "Give me a phone call if it don't show up," he say to us. But we never need to 'cause it was there by nine o'clock the next day.

Ballard do some serious talking to us as we leave.

"Whatever I do is gonna be unpopular with the white people, but I'm gonna have to do things that Indians won't like either, but I'm gonna do what I think is right. I just want you to know that."

"Humff!" Mad Etta snort again when she hear that. "That guy Jesus that the Catholics talk about was right but look where it got him. Ballard'll likely get himself done the same way only today they use government forms instead of nails. Ballard has got himself up in the front line of things, there you got to be popular. Right don't matter a damn."

What Ballard started to do was look at the way the Indian tribes who were handling their own money was spending it. What he see he don't like and he talk to the newspapers

45

about it.

Ballard is then on the television and in the newspapers looking innocent and serious at the same time; they aren't always kind to Ballard and a lot of the stories have some Indian chief saying how Ballard he betraying his own people. One time when I'm alone in Edmonton I drop in to thank him for the wheelchair and he talk a lot to me.

"I've had to change my mind about a lot of things," he say. "There need to be close records kept on each reserve of how all the money is spent. It's not that Indians ain't smart, it's that they don't have any experience handling more than a few dollars at a time. Silas, what would you do if I gave you $5 million to spend on improving the reserve, creating jobs and things like that?"

"I don't know," I say.

"Neither does anyone else. You're one of the smartest young fellows on the reserve, but you'd need some help from white men like bankers and accountants to get projects started, and if you got bad advice or crooked white men, why you'd be in a lot of trouble. I can't see that there is anything wrong with changing my mind. I mean you may be really excited by monkeys in picture-books but when you get close to them you find out they smell bad, bite and got fleas."

Strange thing is that as soon as Ballard was gone, the Alberta Native Brotherhood elect as its President a man named Joe Wood, who be not only a friend of Chief Tom's, but be married to a white lady and live in the city. In less time than you can imagine, the Alberta Native Brotherhood become just another do-nothing group, and you never see their name in the paper with stories and pictures like when Ballard ran them.

Also Ballard he make an investigation and zoom in on how the money being spent here at Hobbema and he find out that there be nine companies formed, all with Chief

46

Tom Crow-eye and his girlfriend, Samantha Yellowknees as directors, and that between the two of them they handling over $3 million, and that most of it gone someplace but not to us Indians.

"You know the reason they agree to give me this job, Silas? They didn't expect me to do anything. Well, I'm gonna do . . ." and we get interrupted by his phone before he tell me more.

One afternoon we hear some strange-funny news on the radio. The announcer laughed while he is reading it, but if it is funny, it is sad-funny. "Ballard Longbow," the newsman say, "the Director General of Indian Affairs for the Province of Alberta, took action today to move the offices of six of his senior advisors to the basement of the Edmonton building they occupy. 'It's time they found out what it's like to be a minority with no rights and a substandard place to work. They'll be better people for it,' Longbow is quoted as saying."

After hearing that news on the radio we borrow Louis Coyote's pickup truck and about a dozen of us head up to Edmonton. We go right up to the CN Tower Building where Ballard have his office.

"You tell Ballard Longbow his friends is here to see him," Frank say to the pink-faced secretary who wear a baggy dress the colour of blue ink.

Her nose get thinner and whiter as she look out over us.

"Whom shall I say is calling?"

"Just tell Ballard he got friends out here or we move *you* down to the basement all by ourselves." As Frank start to move around the desk that secretary lady disappear real fast.

We all give a big cheer when Ballard come walking down the hall.

"It's no big deal," Ballard tells us. "They wouldn't do what I told them. So we'll see who's boss."

47

It seem to me a tough way to do things. In less than six months Ballard has made enemies of most of the Indian Chiefs, a lot of the Indians and all of the white men. He been moving Indian Agents around the province like they was pins in a map.

"Everybody knows that most of the Indian Agents are incompetent. Everybody knows that bands all over Alberta have wasted millions and millions of dollars. Everybody knows that some of the minor officials and some of the Indians are crooks. Everybody knows all these things, but there is a big difference between knowing and getting proof that the RCMP can take to court. It's gonna take years for the RCMP to investigate in all the places I've told them to. But, boy, I'm gonna nail a lot of tails to the wall, even if it takes a few years to do."

Over the next few days we hear it all on the radio and TV. The Minister of Indian Affairs in Ottawa tell Ballard to move them white men up from the basement. Ballard say either he is the boss of Alberta or not and he send off a letter to Ottawa that get printed up in the newspaper and read over the television. It is addressed to The Great White Father: "I have humbly received your edict not to move your brothers to the basement . . ." is how it start off.

"It's dripping with sarcasm and irony," Mr. Nichols say when I talk to him about it. He explain them to me but I'm still not sure if they're good or bad.

In another day or two, Ballard he is fired from his job. His assistants get moved back upstairs, the Indian Agents go back to where they always been, and guys like Chief Tom breathe a lot easier. In a week or so the newspapers all get tired of the story and nobody hear of Ballard Longbow no more.

He go back to working as a counsellor in Edmonton like he did before. RCMP either stop investigate the way money been spent or else say nobody done nothing intentional wrong.

Last Saturday Ballard show up in the evening to the dance at Blue Quills Hall. He smile when he see me and we have a cup of coffee and talk for a while.

"I done what I told everybody never to do. I trusted *them*. I believed *them* when they said I could accomplish more working with them than against them." He raise up his fists like he going to bring them down hard on the table we sitting at in the hall kitchen, but he don't. Instead he take a deep breath and make a small smile at me.

"Think I'll give a little talk at the intermission when the band take their break. Like Mad Etta said about me, I'm gonna have to ride around the edges and pick them off one at a time. Think I'll start with Joe Wood and the Alberta Native Brotherhood, election coming up soon."

At intermission Ballard get up and start to talk. It don't seem very exciting anymore or even funny. "I've heard all this before," Frank Fence-post say. "Let's go outside to the truck and have a beer." Most people have the same idea and as they push toward the door, I hear that Ballard is telling that story about the Peigan dog.

BUFFALO JUMP

When we get there he give to me his cigarettes and matches, a couple of dollars and a jackknife with a white pearl handle that have little roses set in it, look like they growing out of a snow bank.

"Silas, you and Sadie have a couple of beers on me," he say, and his face make the motions of a smile though there ain't nothing behind it. The knife feel light and smooth in my hand like a real worn coin. Ever since I met Gooch I always liked that knife. I know that's not what I should be thinking about but it is.

"What did you tell everybody?" Gooch ask as I unload his wheelchair from the back of the truck.

"Etta was the only one who asked and I told her I was taking you with me to pick sweetgrass."

Where I have stopped the truck is near the top of a buffalo jump way at the back end of the Ermineskin Reserve, maybe ten miles from Hobbema, the town where we live.

Gooch put his good arm on the passenger door and swing down to the ground. His legs lay in front of him, floppy as a doll's. Gooch used to be over six foot tall. His left arm be limp like it made of rubber and he have to reach across and lift it with his right arm when he want to move it. Gooch got himself shot up pretty bad a couple of years ago. Now he has to push himself around with the one arm that be strong, I bet, as four men.

"Knowing you, Silas, I suppose I better pick some sweet-grass so I don't make you out to be a liar," he say, as he shove himself along to the back of the truck. He don't let me help him, but pull himself up into the chair all by his lonesome. He's right. I don't much like to lie, especially to other Indians. Picking sweetgrass easy for Gooch to do 'cause the ground be covered with it. The air, too, is full of the lemon-spicy smell of it.

Gooch pick himself some big handfuls of sweetgrass, stuff the stems under his left arm, then with his right hand he divide the grass into parts and with his big, long fingers he braid that grass up tight as little girls' pig tails. It amaze me to see him do that. I can't braid rope even with my two good hands.

"Mad Etta told me to come back with a good supply, so pick as much as you like," I say.

Gooch ain't one of us. He is a Tlingit Indian come all the way from Alaska. Couple of years ago in summer he come walking into the pool-hall at Hobbema, rough and laughing and full of life. He give off energy like heat from a stove. Within a day he got himself a woman, Sandra Coyote, and made himself more friends than I ever had or likely will have. But he make himself one enemy, too, Sandra's boyfriend, Paul Cutknife.

Paul is off in prison at Prince Albert, got ten years for kill Sandra and the baby she had inside her and for wound Gooch.

Some say the RCMP forgot about sending him back to Alaska, while some others say they wouldn't take him. Pretty hard for one government to get another to take a crippled Indian. Anyway, he live on with Sandra's people. I don't know if Gooch is a first or last name. Somebody, probably me, ask him one day, but all he say as an answer is, "Was Geronimo a first or last name?"

It is bad business we got out here at the buffalo jump, but I don't know how to stop it or even if I should. Gooch hand me the sweetgrass braid. "You burn this and think of me the next time there be a Sundance Ceremony," he say. And I think of the warm, sweet smoke that is waved over the dancers at a sundance. Sweetgrass is considered sacred because it grows all over the country but horses and cattle never eat it.

What Gooch has decided to do is die.

After the hospital fixed him up as good as they could they send him back to the reserve. It sure make me sad to see the way he is crippled, especially to see dragging sideways on the ground, his boots, what be a buckskin colour, soft as suede and have silver toe-caps.

I can only imagine what it must be like for a guy like Gooch who walk loud, live hard and happy, to lose his woman, his legs and an arm, all at one time.

We aren't surprised that he be awful depressed and just lay on a bed in Coyote's cabin, but what do surprise us is that he won't let Mad Etta doctor on him.

"I don't want to see her," is all he say, and he won't let us take him to her cabin, or let her come up to Coyote's to look at him.

We do take him into town with us a couple of times. Me and Frank or his friends, Robert and Eathen want to carry him but he says, no way, and push along on the ground, joke that he dragging his ass like a bitch in heat. But he don't joke for long. Beer don't make him happy like we figured and when he see people out on the dance floor, stomp up a storm, it just make him sadder than he ever been. Gooch was about the best dancer there ever was. "He can make you feel sexy and important just by the way he dance with you,"

I remember Sandra saying to me one time.

I talk a lot about him to Mad Etta our medicine lady. Etta is so good a doctor that once in a while a white man come around the reserve ask for a cure for his rheumatism, or something for a sick kid that white doctors can't help. Etta is learning me some of the business of being a medicine man.

"You know what the toughest thing is about doing medicine?" Etta ask, then answer herself, I guess 'cause she don't expect me to know. "All your patients is gonna die someday. Don't matter how much good you do for them—it be like stretching out one of them rubber bands—you can only stretch it so far before it snap and disappear into nothing."

"Kind of like holding off a whole pack of wolves with only a willow switch," I say. Etta's old, dark eyes look harsh at me, but finally she nod her head. "You figure you could help Gooch if you was to doctor on him?" I go on.

"He ain't asked."

"That ain't what I asked."

"To cure people they got to believe in you."

"Gooch have lots of pride. It be hard for him to ask." Etta just shrug her buffalo-big shoulders. We is both silent for a long time.

But Gooch never ask. He just sit around, sad as a spoiled apple.

That's why we decide a nice thing to do would be to get a wheelchair for Gooch. Me and my friends figure to do it by creative borrowing and the best way we can think of is to take Gooch to the hospital and then just wheel him away when we get the chance.

We first asked Mr. Ernest Paul, a BC Indian who supposed to do some kind of social-work job for Indian Affairs Department, if he can get us a wheelchair. He give us about a hundred forms to fill out. We afraid to tell the truth that Gooch ain't Cree or Canadian, so we leave an awful lot of

53

blanks when we turn the forms back to him.

"It take six months or a year before you hear," he tell us.

"Hell, anybody can make a baby in nine months, shouldn't take that long for a wheelchair," says Frank Fence-post. We sure don't want to wait that long 'cause we pretty sure the answer be no anyway.

One afternoon we load Gooch up in Louis Coyote's pick-up truck and drive to the hospital in Wetaskiwin. We take him in the emergency door and he say that his left arm hurt him real bad. They put him in a wheelchair while he wait for a doctor to see him, but boy, the nurses there watch us like hawks, even after Gooch been examined and we say we just push him out to the truck and come right back quick. They let us push him to the truck, but a big orderly come along to return the chair.

It is now kind of a challenge for us to get a chair like we said we would. So me and my friend Frank Fence-post, his girl Connie Bigcharles, my girl Sadie One-wound, Eathen and Rufus Firstrider, Robert and Bedelia Coyote, sit around for a couple of hours and make us up a plan. Bedelia Coyote who is Robert's sister, and was Sandra's sister too, is good at making plans. First thing she say we have to do is drive up to Edmonton.

When she hear what we is going for, Molly Cheekbone come along too. Molly is taking a nursing-aid course down to the Tech School in Wetaskiwin and she would sure like to do some practising on Gooch. And I know she been over to Coyote's cabin to see him a few times.

"You know," Gooch he say to me one day, "it funny that even though my legs be no good to me, I can still . . . you know . . . make babies," and he blush as much as an Indian is able, and his face break into a big smile like he just done something to be really proud of. It seem strange to me that Gooch, who always be one for use the strong language, get all embarrassed by something like that. Guess the bullets in him must have dulled his tongue too. I say something to him about that but he just keep grinning like he maybe discovered a spring that give out Lethbridge Pale Ale instead of water. But after a while he even turn that happiness around the wrong way.

First place we stop in Edmonton be the Indian Friendship Centre and we find out from Dave Smallface, the manager there, the name of an Indian patient in one of the big hospitals. It turn out to be the University Hospital, so we drive over there and visit the lady whose name is Vera Bellgrade.

What Bedelia Coyote has made us do is bring along our guitars and she gone and dressed me up to look more like a cowboy than I ever been before. I'm wearing a borrowed ten-gallon hat, Eathen's red-and-white cowboy chaps, and carrying about a hundred feet of rope coiled over my arm.

The nurses and people in the halls sure look at us funny. One old man in a green dressing-gown turn his head right around in a full circle after me. "I'm gonna do some trick roping," I say, and throw a lasso at one of them tall silver ashtrays full of sand that stand in hallways. I hit the side of it and tip it right over.

"Be careful," say Bedelia who have a voice like a school teacher.

Turn out that the Indian lady, Vera Bellgrade, be an Athabasca Indian who don't speak English or Cree, so she sure must wonder why her room is all of a sudden full of strange Indians with guitars. We smile a lot at her and Eathen strum his guitar and sing some songs by Charlie Pride and Eddy Rabbit, what we all heard on the radio.

We intentional make so much noise that a nurse come down and ask us to close up the door. We do, but first we haul in from the hall a couple of wheelchairs, say to the nurse that they is for people to sit on. She grumble about too many visitors at one time but don't say we can't. Soon as she goes we fold up one of the chairs and I tie my rope to it and we lower it out of the window to where Sadie One-wound and Molly Cheekbone is waiting. We are on the fourth floor and when we let the rope out all the way, Sadie and Molly, even when they jump can't reach the chair. We don't want to let it fall in case it break, so Robert Coyote, who is the tallest of us, quick run outside and with Molly stand up on his shoulders, guide it to the ground. We all cheer and sing some more songs for the sick lady. Only English she seem to know how to say is, "Crazy buggers," and she say it quite a few times, shake her head and smile.

Even that nice chair don't make Gooch as happy as we would like. And when, a month or so later, Molly Cheekbone say she want to move in with him, that don't cheer him up either, and he don't let her; tell her go find a man that got all his parts working.

After he is sick, Gooch and me get to be closer friends than we ever was before. He used to always be with Sandra and he run too with Robert and Eathen who is tough dudes and don't always have time for me because they think I'm funny for writing things down the way I do.

I bring for Gooch books to read, the ones I like, about Indian history and the old ways of our people. He leave the first ones lay around until they is maybe a month overdue at the library but eventually he get tired of just sitting and he read them. In the evenings we talk about the old customs but Gooch has his mind set mainly on death and dying.

"I read about the way they bury dead warriors in the old days," he say. "I want you should follow some of them customs when I'm gone, Silas. Used to be a Worthy Man of the tribe would cut off a lock of the dead brave's hair and tie it to a stick what was stuck in the ground by the grave and left for four days."

56

I nod to show that I know what he is talking about.

"Then they bring the stick and lock back to camp and the Worthy Man pray to Manitou to let the braid become a spirit so that when the braid be put into a bundle and is spoken to, it answer. I think that sound like fun," and Gooch grin that big, gap-toothed smile of his for about the second time since he was shot. "I kind of like the idea of being in a medicine bundle and of talking to people. Boy, if I talked from a medicine bundle I'd sure curl the hair of some of the people we know," and Gooch come right out and laugh, but it is about as unhappy as a laugh can be.

"I'm like an old lady, Silas," Gooch say another time. "I read the books, and Molly take me down to Blue Quills Hall and I sit with the ladies, learn how to do the weaving and macrame stuff. God, man, I'm used to driving a bulldozer," and he slap his good hand on the arm of the wheelchair.

I remember one time in the bar of the Alice Hotel in Wetaskiwin this big white man got interested in Sandra Coyote. Sandra was really pretty and that night she was wearing a red satin blouse and tight jeans that showed off all the right parts of her.

We was sitting close to a table of truckers and one guy about 45 with a barrel chest and beer belly make remarks about Sandra a couple of times, then as she get up to go buy cigarettes, he pat her ass as she walk past his table. Gooch is out of his chair and around the table all in one movement and he pull the big guy to his feet and spin him around. Gooch is standing tall between the tables, his head thrown back and a half-smile on his face. His muscles bulge like links of logging chain where he got the sleeves of his purple shirt rolled up, and he wear an open denim vest over that shirt. He remind me of a stallion you see gallop across a pasture. He is tough and free and smell of life.

That big trucker raise up his fist to Gooch, but he don't

57

throw it—it is almost like he been hit though—he just look at Gooch and sense that he be in big trouble if he keep on.

"Go ahead, partner," Gooch say to him. "Let only fear and common sense stop you," and he grin but he got his eyes glued to the trucker's eyes in case he make a quick move. The trucker sit down and him and his friends pretend that they is really interested in their beer.

I wonder where *that* Gooch is gone to?

"Molly's the best, man, but what can I do for her? I lay here like a sleeping woman while she climb on top of me. I don't feel like a man no more."

Frank, he suggest we should hook up some ropes and pulleys over Gooch's bed so he could get into the right position for sex. "Hell, it would be just like landing one of them helicopters," says Frank. Gooch, he pretend he gonna punch Frank's nose for him, but anyone can see the idea tickles him.

Somebody say then that it is a bad idea for Frank to make jokes about somebody who be handicapped the way Gooch is. It is about the only time I see Frank get really mad.

"We can't go around with long faces the way white people do. If Gooch was white, his handicap would make him equal to an Indian. If we don't laugh at ourselves, we is all gonna die."

But Gooch don't get no happier and he finally decide he is going to help himself to die and he trust me to take him out to this here buffalo jump where he figure to drop over the edge. "I just roll my chair down to the very edge and then push myself off with my good arm here."

"You know," I say, holding on to the sweetgrass braid he just made, "if you was to look at those sweetgrass stems you're holding, as you and your friends . . . we could make, by braiding together, a pretty solid life for all of us. We don't mind helping you. . . ." Gooch screw up his face and I know I just sounded like one of the priests or even Chief Tom. I

58

suppose it was worth a try though. I seen a guy do something like that with silk threads at a union meeting in Wetaskiwin once.

I decide to try another line.

"Hey, you remember what Etta says? 'Only the rocks live forever. It don't matter how long you live but how....'" Boy, I think I said the wrong thing, but I had the good intentions. I was trying to get him to think about living, not dying. "She also say, 'It's not the size of the dog in the fight, it's the size of the fight in the dog!'" though I don't know what that has to do with anything. It gonna be a long time before I'm able to be a medicine man all by myself.

"Etta don't know so much."

"Is that why you never let her doctor on you? You know she done wonderful cures for other people."

"Sure, she just stuff me full of that skunk-smelling stuff she cooks up and I'll grow new legs and arms just like a potato been left in the cellar too long."

"You could let her try. It's better than killing yourself."

"If she don't do no good, what have I got to look forward to then?"

"Same as now." Gooch get mad at that and wheel his chair up out of the hollow it been sitting in, toward the edge of the buffalo jump. He go over a little bump and roll real fast just like he been pushed down a ramp. One time not long after Gooch got his chair, we set the door off One-wound's outhouse against the back of the truck, same as when we load Mad Etta up to take her someplace. Then me, Frank, Gooch, Eathen, Robert, Emmanuel Monoose and a few others have us a contest, see who can roll the wheelchair furthest. We line up with our backs against the cab of the truck and then wheel for all we worth until we hit the ramp, then coast as far as we can. Funny, but Gooch with only his one good arm beat us all by about ten feet.

Seen from down below, before we drove up the long hill to get to the top, the buffalo jump look like a hairy green tongue stick out of the mouth of the earth. The drop from the top must be 50 feet or more and it is not just onto a meadow, but onto the rocks of what used to be a creek bed. In the old days Indians would steer buffalo toward the hill and then stampede them over the jump. Sure beat killing them one at a time with arrows or even guns.

I've tried all that I know to do. I shake Gooch's hand and pretend to act brave. "I'll just sit here for a while in the sun before I make the trip," he say. "You don't tell nobody for two days. Then you come out and pick up the chair. You can bury me, or put me out on a platform. Whatever you do is okay with me."

I am about five steps away, my heart feeling like it weigh a hundred pounds inside me when I hear Gooch call.

"Hey, Silas, remember how you told me one time about the old days you Crees used to kill a man's favourite horse after he died so's his spirit wouldn't have to walk. . . ?"

"What do you want me to do . . . smash up this here wheelchair?"

"Hell, no . . . I don't figure to need my wheelchair where I'm going, and maybe somebody else be able to use it. But what I'd like you to do for me is that maybe you and Frank, Eathen and Robert, could kill off one of them $20,000 vans what got pictures all over the outside, velvet seats, a bar and a bed," and his face crack up into a smile and it be so beautiful it just like the kaleidoscope toy my littlest sister got for Christmas from the welfare. We both laugh and Gooch signal me with his good hand to keep walking away while we both smiling.

I sort of stumble into the deep hollow, like a dimple, where Gooch was sitting earlier. "You could make a fire in here if you wanted to," I say.

"With what?" say Gooch turning his good hand palm up to show it empty.

If I go back to Hobbema right away I know I'm going to have to answer a lot of questions from Coyotes and from Molly Cheekbone, so I drive on up to Edmonton and hang around the Indian Friendship Centre for two days.

It is sunny with snowy clouds in the high sky as I drive back to the buffalo jump. As I come up on it from the back I can see the sun glint off Gooch's empty wheelchair, sit way up at the very edge. I would rather, I figure, get the chair first. Time enough to go down to the rocks.

I park the truck and walk slow toward the chair. Then a movement catch my eye. It is from the hollow in the ground. I run the last few steps to it and there is Gooch sit in the hollow, and beside him is I bet a hundred or so sweetgrass braids stacked in a criss-cross way like you pile lumber.

The parts of his face start to rearrange themselves and I can see he got a large smile coming on. I don't know what I am going to say to him but I guess something will come to me.

GOLDIE

Old cowboys is like old cars, broke down most of the time and a lot of expense to whoever own one. Chet Waggoner is an old cowboy, and I never been able to understand why Goldie Sanderson spend most of her life waiting for him.

I seen Chet around the cafe and heard he was Goldie's man, but it never was important until Miss Goldie give me a Saturday-night job, wash the dishes and keep the kitchen clean.

I been going to the Gold Nugget Café in Wetaskiwin most of my life. It sits across the street from the Canadian Legion with the railroad tracks and the UGG elevator behind it. Used to be there was just a small frame house but about the time I was born Miss Goldie took some money that her mama left her and built onto the front of the house, with concrete blocks, the Gold Nugget Café. When you walk in, there be a counter down the right side, six booths covered in dark-green leather stuff on the other wall, and four kitchen tables and chairs scattered around between where the booths and counter end and the kitchen start.

Miss Goldie don't mind having Indians for customers. She treat us like everybody else and don't spend all her time watching to see that we don't steal the knives, forks and ashtrays like they do at the other cafés in Wetaskiwin and

Ponoka.

I don't know how come Goldie Sanderson never got married. At one time or another she could of had most of the men around Wetaskiwin. She must of been only about twenty when she opened up the café, which make her a little less than 40 now. As white ladies go, she is still very pretty. And they say when she was young she was beautiful, though I never noticed 'cause she always seem really old to me. Goldie be tall and slim and have hair that's naturally the colour of red plums. She wear that hair upswept most times, with a gold or green scarf in it. She told me that she one time took a course from one of those women who sell make-up and now she always wears the right kind of rouge and eyeshadow to make her look pretty but not hard.

"I'm getting my second chance at all these guys," she say to me one day after I hear Mr. Calkins, who have the Gulf Oil Bulk Station, ask her to a show and dance at the Elks Club. He lean over the back of me, where I sitting at the counter, to ask, and he talk right through me like I wasn't there at all. He is fat, bald, wear his green coveralls with his first name over the pocket in red thread. He is sweating and wring his hands together while he ask. Goldie say no to him in a nice way so he don't go away mad. When he's gone she say, "When I was young these same guys used to chase after me. Eventually they all got married and had families, now they're getting divorced, or just antsy, and they come nosing around here the way dogs crawl flat on their bellies when they want something. If I didn't need their coffee business I'd run them right out of the place. Hell, I didn't want them when they were young, why would I want them now?" and she laugh and pour herself a cup of coffee.

I sure would like to ask why she been Chet Waggoner's woman when she could of done lots better. I heard once that Dr. McCall who own the whole Wetaskiwin Medical Arts

63

Building proposed to her one time. I mean Chet don't even live with her steady.

"Shiftless" is the word people use to describe Chet Waggoner. Even at the Canadian Legion, and Alice Hotel beer parlour, they say that about him. Chet is what most people would picture when somebody say cowboy: short, got a chest like a tame rooster, but is wiry and lean with eyes deep in his face and squinted always like he looking into a strong sun.

Chet is away all the summers on the rodeo circuit and used to be in the winters he went off to the United States, I guess to places like Nevada or Arizona where it is always warm. He never been much of a success, though I guess he had most of his bones broke at one time or another. Last couple of winters he stayed around Wetaskiwin, sat in the corner opposite the juke-box, his cowboy hat tipped back on his head, drink coffee and roll cigarettes from the package of Bull Durham in the pocket of his western shirt.

It is September now and he come back a week or so ago in the worst shape I ever seen him. His camper truck died somewheres, or he had to sell it, or more likely the finance company come and got it. He arrive back in Wetaskiwin on the north-bound bus, packing his saddle and a duffle bag, and with a cast on one foot.

"I'll be back on the circuit in a couple of weeks," he says, and winks at whoever listening to him. "Only way you can kill a cowboy is to cut off his head and then hide it."

I've never liked Chet very much. He is sullen and quiet most of the time, even when he been drinking which is also most of the time. His voice is kind of whiny and when he tries to make jokes they aren't very funny, like when he calls me Number Nine, which come from a country song, *Engine, Engine, Number Nine*, I think sung by Roger Miller. He also tell over and over a story about how he missed being all-round cowboy at the Calgary Stampede by only one point.

He is not like Goldie who kid with us just like we were regular people.

"You got any buffalo burgers?" my friend Frank Fence-post will say to her. "No more junk food for us Indians— from now on we eat natural."

"Get out of here Fence-post, you wouldn't know a buffalo if one walked up and shook hands with you. But I tell you what, I've got some moosemeat in the freezer that's been there for about ten years. Should be just about right for a tough Indian like you. How do you want it, raw?"

"Maybe we should put off this natural-food idea for another day. How about you bring me some french fries with gravy, a Coke and some soft ice cream."

"Bring it to him all in one bowl," I say. "It gonna get mixed up in his stomach anyway." And everybody have a good laugh.

Last Saturday I come into town early before I due to go to work at five o'clock, stop at the café for lunch, and go shop in the stores for a present for my girlfriend Sadie One-wound who have a birthday soon. Sadie is awful special to me. She like to hold on to me, and I guess we'd do about anything try to make each other happy.

I was sure surprised when Miss Goldie offer me the part-time job here at the café. I guess she like me because I try to be polite, and too, I try to keep Frank Fence-post from do too many awful things like change the sugar for salt and fill up the napkins with salt so that when people shake them out they get a shower.

"She's tough as boiled owl shit," I've heard people say about Goldie, and it true that she can swear like a cowhand and I seen her back drunks out the door, matching them cuss for cuss. But she is not one to do things like that if it ain't necessary, and when she do she have a way about her like a

65

mother bird defending her nest.

One good thing about Chet is that when he's around he do all the repairs for the café. One winter he paint the whole inside of the restaurant, and in the spring he do all the outside of both the café and the house. He fix up the toilets in the washrooms so's they don't run all the time and put down new tiles on the kitchen floor. He start quite a few times to fix up the gate from the backyard to the alley but somehow that is one job that never get done.

"Bugger, he's been gonna fix that gate for five years at least," Miss Goldie say one day while we unloading supplies from the wholesale from the back seat of her car.

"I'll do it for you," I say.

"No. It'll keep. I'll get after him in the spring."

But the spring come and went, the gate don't get fixed, and Chet be off to rodeo again.

One of the years when Chet was doing pretty good he got himself a new Fargo one-ton with a camper. The camper have a bucking horse on the side of it and the Fargo have a big silver windscreen come way up above the hood. I remember us kids seeing it parked in front of the Gold Nugget Café and stand around counting the butterflies and bumblebees what got squashed into the silver-painted mesh. He have printed signs on the back of the camper say things like, "Pass quickly—driver chews tobacco," and, "Cowboys make better lovers."

"I'm looking for a stake," I hear Chet say one day about three weeks ago. "Going to pick up the circuit at the Tucson Indoor. I know where I can get me a GMC pickup with a small camper for $300 down, and I need food and entry fee money, $1500 will do me. I'm gonna go see Jack Reynolds down at the feed mill. He's staked me before."

Jack Reynolds be about Chet's age, which I'd guess at 40, and he own a feed lot, mill and store. He wear an expensive western suit and smoke cigars, have a big house about a mile out of town and drive three or four new cars. He used to ride a little rodeo years ago and been known to stake young cowboys in return for half their prize money. Chet sure ain't a young cowboy: he be in about the same condition as the pickup he wants to buy, all faded, covered in dents and scrapes with over a hundred thousand miles on him. I don't figure he stands much of a chance with Jack Reynolds.

In fact a friend of mine, Dolphus Youngbear, was in the feed store and hear part of the argument: just Chet and Jack coming out of Jack's office with Chet really mad and Jack putting an arm on his shoulders and telling him to give up the rodeo 'cause he be too old for it anymore. Dolphus say Jack offer a job at the feed lot but Chet just go hobbling off on his one boot and one plaster foot.

What I bought Sadie is a useless thing I wouldn't buy unless it was her birthday and something she'd never buy for herself. She seen it at the Metropolitan Store in Wetaskiwin: a necklace of what I would call play Indian jewellery. It is some balls of robin-egg-blue plastic with yellow feathers glued to them. It looks awful but if it makes Sadie's heart feel good to have it, then I get it for her. That, I think, is what love is partly about: doing harmless things for somebody you like, even though you don't understand why.

Chet is pretty downhearted for a few days. He sit over at the Canadian Legion for a lot of the afternoons drinking beer and then sit quiet at his table in the café in the evenings. He still call me Number Nine, but also can kid me about going to the Technical School here at Wetaskiwin. "Hell, when I was a boy I had to ride fifteen miles to school, bareback on a pinto pony, just like an Indian. You any idea how many sideroads there are in fifteen miles?" he ask, to explain why he never got past the fifth grade.

It is while I am having lunch that Chet come back from

the doctor's office with the cast off his foot and holding a fistful of bills. "Be leaving day after tomorrow," he says. "Jack Reynolds changed his mind like I always knew he would. I'm going to sign the papers for the truck and camper in about an hour. Hell, Chet Waggoner's promises don't take funny bounces. You can take my word to the bank."

Goldie, when she hear, give him a hug and a kiss, say she is really happy for him, and I think she is.

When I get to work after my shopping for Sadie's present the café be really busy and the dishes from all afternoon is piled up in the kitchen. I'm just getting started when Goldie stick her face in the square hole where the food get passed to the restaurant. "Silas, run into the office, please. In the top drawer of the desk you'll find a big chequebook. Open it up and there will be a cheque all made out to Gray Beverages. Tear it out and bring it to me."

To get to the office I have to go out the back door of the café and across the yard to the back door of the house and inside to a spare bedroom been made into an office. On the way I step over the new lumber and hinge Chet laid out on the sidewalk, all ready to fix the gate. The gate to the alley hang crooked, remind me of a broken wrist I seen one time, and the old boards is weathered to the soft colour of owl feathers.

I pull open the desk drawer and take out the chequebook which be full of big, bright blue cheques from the Bank of Montreal. The cheque to Gray Beverages is there. The thing that catch my eye though is the bank balance on the cheque stub which be about ten times what I ever imagined Miss Goldie would have in the bank, and above it, I see that the second-last cheque what was wrote was for $1800 to Jack Reynolds.

That puzzle me more than anything I can think of. It must be that she's putting up the money for Chet. But why?

Late that night, when I'm finished cleaning the kitchen, I say goodnight to Miss Goldie, turn off the lights and leave by the back door. I get only as far as the gate when I remember I forgot Sadie's present. I go back in quiet, pick it up, then take a quick look into the café.

Goldie has turned off the sign outside and the lights inside, and sat down at Chet's table, low on her chair with her feet straight out in front. I can't see Chet from where I am but I can just make out the shape of Goldie's white uniform and see the red glow of her cigarette in the dark. There are a few golden threads of light from a streetlight way across by the Legion, and the room look like it full of leafy shadows. The only other light is from the juke-box, yellow where the names of the records is lit up, and moving blues and reds where bubbles swim through the rainbow-shaped coloured tubes of the machine.

It is absolutely quiet—Goldie and Chet don't know I'm there and if I move now, they'll see me standing with my face looking out of the slot where the food orders are set up, like I was an Indian on a television screen. I stay quiet. I hear Chet scrape his chair back from the table and see him walk in that bow-legged way of his, over to the juke-box. He is all dressed in denim and the inkiness of him blocks my view of the juke-box and darkens the room even more. He digs in the front pocket of his jeans and after a while comes out with a handful of coins—one drops on the floor and he cusses soft under his breath, while the coin rolls for a long time, can't tell in what direction. Chet plop money into the machine and stand stooped over it making up his mind. He turn a little to the side and the light show his one cheek golden, skin tight as if it were stretched over a drum.

The machine click way down inside and the first record come on; it is Sammy Smith sing *Help Me Make It Through the Night*. Chet push two more buttons and then scuff his way back to the table, but instead of sitting down his dark shape stop in front of Miss Goldie and I'm pretty sure he bow a little to her. I can't see his face as she look up at him but I wish I could. She stand up then, put herself into his arms, and they dance, real slow and close, like it was the home-going waltz at Blue Quills Hall on a Saturday night.

Chet pulls her up to him, whisper some in her ear and she move herself even closer to him. The way he holds her is not hard, like a man who needs a woman for sex, but like a man who needs to be held as much as she does. This sure ain't the Chet Waggoner everyone knows. Guess he saves this soft side of himself for only Goldie to see. I've always thought of Miss Goldie as big, and Chet as small, but when they dance her head fit nice onto his shoulder and in the dark they be like one person, dark and light all stirred together.

I been grip Sadie's present so hard that I got the box all bent, now as the music get loud toward the end of the song, I move careful to the back door and close it quiet after me. I think I understand now something that happened in the afternoon. When I first seen the new lumber and hinge to repair the gate, laying there on the sidewalk, I figured I could do that job in fifteen minutes or less. I went out to Louis Coyote's pickup truck, got a hammer and screwdriver, and was about to start when Miss Goldie stuck her head out the back door.

"Don't you dare," she said. "Chet will fix that gate, or it will just have to wait until he's ready."

THE CHICKEN DANCER

Fred Visitor claim he going to kill Carson Longhorn and Carson got no reason to believe it ain't true. Carson come pounding on the door to my room in the Queen's Hotel in Calgary about five o'clock in the morning. When I finally let him in he look all around careful to make sure we is alone before he take a quick step inside and at the same time look over his shoulder. He let out a long sigh then tighten up again quick when he catch sight of the lump under the covers over to one side of the bed. He look at me with one scared look all over his face.

"It's Sadie," I tell him. Just then the lump move a little bit and her slim brown hand peek out from under the covers and make with a little wave in our direction. There is lots of us Indians from Hobbema down here for the Calgary Stampede. Me and my girlfriend, Sadie One-wound, ain't here for no special reason except to look around. Not like Carson Longhorn. Him and a bunch of other Cree Indians from our reserve do dancing on the outdoor stage in the infield across from the grandstand every night.

Carson is little and skinny, sink-chested and hollow-cheeked. He got thin black hair that is long and hang over his face like some of them purebred dogs rich people lead around. He only come up to about my armpit, but boy, when he get turned loose to dance he go around that stage like a motorcycle. He is the best chicken dancer ever to come from our reserve and he is always winning prizes and trophies when a bunch of reserves get together for pow-wows and dance contests.

"I sneak uptown here by the side streets, take me most of the night. Fred Visitor carrying a rifle and he going to kill me. All his friends is looking for me too," Carson says, and he go to the window, peek out from behind the yellowed lace curtain to where the sun is just kind of a pink stain way off in the east. If we was in the country birds would be singing this time of day, but here in the city morning sounds be of trucks and cars move along the narrow street. We had the window open and even in the morning you can smell car exhaust and french fries cooking.

I don't figure I have to ask Carson why Fred Visitor is want to kill him. Fred got a pretty wife name of Caroline who don't mind spreading her body around. Even though I think she got good reasons for what she does, if her husband disagree that make him right because he is about one of the meanest dudes I know.

"On account of Caroline?" I say, just to be sure. Carson nod.

"It ain't the way you think though," he say. "Me and Caroline we gonna stay together permanent. If Fred don't catch me and kill me."

I look at him, kind of lift my eyebrows up, make my eyes wide. My face must look to him like a question mark, 'cause he smile at me in a kind of embarrassed but proud way.

Sadie has stuck her head up from under the covers. "You keep Caroline Visitor happy you must of been named right," she say, and reach out for a cigarette from the package on the little stand by the bed.

Carson look all embarrassed again. "It's Fred bring on

all his own trouble," he say. "He hardly ever want his woman. Caroline need a man every day or more."

I know that what he say is true. I had her one time. It was a Saturday night dance at Blue Quills Hall at Hobbema. I went outside to get some air. Was raining pretty hard and I was standing under the eaves watching the rain drip and having a cigarette when Caroline come along. Like me, she been dancing hard for most of the evening. She still breathing fast when she stop beside me.

"That dancing kind of hard work," I say. Caroline look up at me for a second, kind of shiver and toss her beautiful long hair off her face, at the same time check to see if anyone watching. Then she just push her belly up against me and put her mouth inside mine, and make herself hot as noon sun all over my body. She take my hand and we skip across the gravel parking-lot to where her and Fred's camper is parked, and we climb inside. Caroline is one pretty lady. Her hair is blue-black and shine in the sun like a crow wing. She got full lips, shiny white teeth and a nice built body.

Caroline is wearing little black shoes which she kick off quick. She drop her jeans and ain't wearing nothing under them. She open up the front of her scarlet blouse and lie back on the bed. Her breasts seem to be a darker brown than she is and the nipples is pointy and the colour of brown suede. As soon as I get my clothes off she pull me inside her. She grab my shoulders like they was a chicken-wire fence and she was gonna fall ten storeys if she was to let go. Her body get stiff and seem to push me up in the air the way an inflating inner tube might. She make little screams and bite at my tongue. Then she let out a lot of breath and sink down to her regular size and it easy to tell she feeling better.

"I don't want you should think bad of me, Silas," Caroline say to me while we having a cigarette. "Fred never want me anymore. It just that sometimes I have to . . . you know . . ."

73

"Don't have to explain," I tell her, and go on to say I real happy she picked me 'cause I always seen how pretty she was and wished I would make love with her. We do it one more time before I leave, and she say, "Thank you, Silas," to me and give me a big smile. "Anytime," I tell her.

Carson has been talking while I been thinking. "It sure funny that a little skinny guy like me able to outdo a guy like Fred when it come to a woman."

It is too, 'cause Fred Visitor be over six foot tall, weight must be 250 pounds. He is wide across the shoulders as a horse across the ass. He bulldogs steers in the rodeos and can lift the back end of a pickup truck off the ground after he's had a few drinks. Him and his friends are one tough bunch, like to drink hard and fist-fight lots especially when they sure of winning.

All I need is to have a scared-to-death Indian hiding in my room for the rest of Stampede week.

"How come you came here?" I ask as if I didn't already know.

"I want you to do something to get me out of this trouble," he say and look up at me like a dog just been caught eating off the table.

I am supposed to be the assistant to Mad Etta who be the medicine lady for our tribe. Etta is back home in Hobbema. I sure do wish she was here, or else that she teached me a whole lot more of her tricks and stuff than she did. It ain't long ago that she decided I was to be her helper and so far about all she's done is let me watch her make up medicine bags or mix up herbs for a poultice. Whenever there is thinking to be done it is always Etta who do it.

I do remember the first thing she told me about being a medicine man and that was, "Never let on when you're scared, or when you don't know what you're doing. Always pretend everything going to be all right even if you're scared

74

as hell."

"I'll see what I can do," I say to Carson in as confident a voice as I can come up with. "Don't figure it should be too hard a problem," and I go to slap Carson Longhorn on the shoulder, maybe make him feel a little good, when all of a sudden I see his face get pale and his eyes big, as he spot something moving over behind the bed.

"It's only Frank," I say, and Carson let out another long sigh, like air hissing out of a tire.

Late in the night we sneaked my best friend, Frank Fence-post and his girlfriend Connie Bigcharles into the room so we wouldn't have to pay for them. They sleeping in a blanket on the floor.

Frank, all sleepy-faced peer at us over top of the bed and hold up Connie's arm to point at the hands on her wristwatch, a five-finger bargain that Frank bought in the Imperial Hotel beer parlour yesterday for $3.

"It's the middle of the night," he say.

When Carson see that Frank ain't an enemy he just keep on talking, "Fred tell all the guys he gonna break up my arms and legs so I never dance again."

"Try not to yell too loud when he does it 'cause I want to get some sleep," says Frank.

"That ain't as bad as it could be," I say. Both Frank and Carson say, "Huh?"

"Last night he was gonna shoot you, probably would of if he'd caught you. But now that he have some time to think and it be daylight and he be sober, all he be looking to do is beat on you."

I explain to Frank and Connie why Carson is hiding in our room.

"Did Fred catch you guys together?" ask Frank.

"No, it was one of his friends, walked right into the camper without knocking. If it been Fred he'd of killed us

75

right there. We knew he was riding in an event over at the Stampede grounds otherwise we wouldn't of been there. I sent Caroline to my sister's place. She be okay there until you straighten this out, Silas."

"There's always a bright side," says Frank from the floor. "Which you like better, dancing or Caroline?"

"Caroline, of course," says Carson.

"Well, look at it this way, if Fred don't tear your cock off you can still fuck even with broken bones," and him and Connie have themselves a good laugh. Carson and me don't figure it is very funny though.

I got ideas bouncing around in my head like corks in a bucket of water, but I can't come up with nothing right then. It make me feel real dumb, 'cause Carson is counting on me. He just sit on a wood chair over in the corner, all bent over and frail-boned like a picture I seen once of a stork. He jump every time a truck go down the alley or somebody slam a door in the hall. Can't blame him too much. It can't be very pleasant to figure you're gonna die soon.

"What can I do?" he keep saying to me. "If he don't shoot me he kill me with his fists. He's twice as big as me. If I get a gun I probably point it the wrong way but even if I was to shoot him it be me that get in trouble."

I have to do something quick I decide.

"If Mad Etta was here would you trust her to get you out of this trouble?"

"Yes."

"Do you trust me?"

"No," he say to the linoleum floor.

"Well, you got a choice of me or nothing," I say, try to make a deep voice. "I got to think on this. We talk about it later," and I turn my back with my arms folded across my chest the way I seen Mad Etta do when she want to end a conversation.

76

I can hear Frank and Connie giggling from behind the bed. Guess I just don't make people believe in me the way Mad Etta does. There is also close to 400 pounds of Mad Etta to back up what she say.

Anyway, I walk out the door with my back straight and like I know where I'm going even though I don't. I go and sit in the Queen's Hotel coffee shop for an hour or so. Drink coffee and think. I try to put myself in everybody's place, see through their face, or as Mad Etta say, walk in their moccasins.

I guess that it is Fred Visitor's pride that been hurt. And lots of times that's worse to a man than a fist in the face or a cut with a knife. He's make it pretty clear that he don't care about Caroline, it just that he's mad to think she go for a fellow like Carson that all the tough men look down on.

Finally I buy up four coffees and a half-dozen doughnuts and take them back up to the room. Everybody is asleep except Carson. He just sit scared and say he don't want no food.

"How well do you and Fred Visitor know each other?" I say. I got this here idea chewing around in my head.

"Hardly at all," say Carson. "I never say more than hello to him a couple of times. You know rodeo guys like him don't have nothing to do with dancers like me."

"That's good," I say. What he say is true too. Used to be that dancers was looked up to by everybody because what they do be just as hard as hunting or rodeoing, but not no more. Rodeo riders and bull ropers is heroes and dancers is kind of figured for sissies. "If you was to have to fist-fight with Fred where is the place you would feel most at home?"

"I—I don't know," say Carson. "He's big . . ."

"On the stage, right?" I say real quick.

"I guess . . ."

"You stay here. I'm gonna go arrange it," and I'm gone

77

out the door before he can say for me not to.

The Crown Hotel beer parlour down near the Stampede grounds is where all the rodeo riders and chuckwagon crews drink. I wait until afternoon before I go there, but not too late, don't want to take a chance that Fred Visitor be drunk and mean. My eyes take a minute or so to get used to the dark of the bar. The place smell like beer and hotel soap. The tables is covered with green towel cloth. It is pretty quiet this time of day and about all I can hear is the clink of glasses and some people laugh quiet.

Fred sitting at a table in the corner with a couple of guys I don't know and a girl named Suzie Calf-robe who be wild as a stray cat, like to drink and fight lots.

"I hear you looking for Carson Longhorn," I say. Fred and his friends look me up and down with mean eyes like maybe I was an RCMP or something bad like that. Finally Fred nod. Then he call Carson all the bad names he can think of and say how good he gonna fix him when he catch him.

"He's ready to settle with you," I say. Boy, I sure hope these dudes don't decide to beat on me in place of Carson, and I wonder if I really want to be Mad Etta's assistant after all.

"How come he don't come himself?" Fred ask and say some more bad things about Carson, how he is a coward and all, like they maybe expect me to defend him.

"He don't want to fight in a bar," I say.

"So where?" says Fred.

"He's gonna fist-fight you right up on the stage in the infield, same one where he does his dancing. No guns or nothing. Just you and him."

"How come there?" says Fred, make a bad face.

"Well," and I lean in close to Fred so to say it like it's almost a secret, "put yourself in his spot. You figure he ever

78

gonna dance again after you get through with him? It be the last time he ever be on a stage."

The time I set for the fight was midnight. I make sure I tell Carson to stay right in the room until it time for us to go. I act like Mad Etta and turn my back on all his arguments for not fist-fighting Fred Visitor. "Once you start something you carry straight on with it," I remember Mad Etta saying. "If you believe in what you doing then so do everyone else."

"You got some money?" I say to Carson, and I ask him for $20. I send Frank and Connie off to find a hardware store and buy two strong flashlights, and I send Sadie out to find my friend Rufus Firstrider and borrow his drum. We all get to the infield an hour early, just after the stage show and dancing finished for the night. The floodlights been turned off and the whole infield, grandstand and racetrack be dark, but a few people walk around just looking at things.

I get them to practise only once what we going to do. It important that Carson think he is going to have to fight. At about quarter to twelve I get everybody in their place. I put Carson up in the middle of the stage in his chicken dancer costume, all bent down in the position he be in to start his dance.

Pretty soon it get to be ten after twelve and all we doing is getting cold. Then I hear voices and I see three guys coming toward the stage. They stop about 50 yards away and Fred Visitor lumber like a big bear up toward me. One of the guys with him is Oscar Stick who be an even meaner fist-fighter than Fred. Oscar is short and tough and I can tell it's him by the way his green-stone belt buckle shine in the dark. If this idea of mine don't work there is going to be more than one busted-up Indian before morning.

Fred sees me standing by the steps to the stage. I take off my hat which is supposed to be a sign to Carson to start one of his rattles shaking, and that shaking be Sadie's sign to start on the drum, and that be Frank and Connie's sign to turn on their lights. I even slap my hat on the edge of the stage a couple of times but still nothing happen.

"Well, where is he?" says Fred, breathing beer in my face.

I point for him to look up on the stage. The way Carson has positioned himself, all bent and squatted, he look in the dark like maybe a pile of old clothes.

Fred stands his big boots on the bottom steps to the stage.

"Dance," I say in a loud whisper, to the lump in the middle of the stage. "Dance," I yell again. I think about running past Fred and giving Carson a good shake to get him started, but about that time Sadie start to beat on the drum. Slow and unsure at first, all the noise probably scare her some, and I don't think she ever played the drum before. Then Frank and Connie turn their flashlights on, shine them right on Carson who still crouch there stupid as a post. Fred must figure we sure making it easy for him.

Just as Fred set his last heavy foot on the stage, Carson finally come to life. He start to shake the calf-skull rattle full of pebbles and he clack together the little metal cymbals he have on his fingers.

Braaack-whirrr, braaack-whirrr they go, make the scary sound of a bird in the bush, and then Carson start to dance a little.

The way Frank and Connie hold the lights, Carson have two or three shadows and they all be about 40 feet tall. He got a yellow bird's beak mask cover the top half of his face and he have mean paint on the rest of his face, arms and chest.

Carson dance round and round, his feet move so fast I can't even follow them. He go so fast his feathers ruffle like there be a strong wind and the chatter of the rattles fill the black air. Finally, at the far side of the stage he turn to show his face to Fred Visitor and as he start toward him he seem to grow to maybe twelve feet tall.

Now it is Fred Visitor's turn to stand to one spot like he grown roots or maybe been nailed to the floor. Coming across the stage Carson be noisy as a train locomotive. When he get to be about ten feet away and maybe twenty feet high, Fred swing on his heel and walk fast down the steps. He mumble something to me about not going to fight no pansy dancer but I can tell he is in one hurry to get away quick.

I bet that back in Hobbema, where Mad Etta sleeping under her bearskin blanket, that she be having good dreams.

THE KILLING OF COLIN MOOSEFEATHERS

We even borrowed a grave for Colin Moosefeathers, which is the way he would of wanted it. Felicien Cyr, the old dude who look after the graveyard on the reserve, like to, especially in the summer months, keep a couple of graves dug ahead of time. It is about 4 AM on what gonna be a hot July day when we is doing the burying. We all been to a party for most of the night and is by now pretty much worse for wear, which is the way Colin would of wanted it too.

On the way out of Wetaskiwin my friend Frank Fencepost he borrow a shovel out of somebody's garden, and him and me and Rufus Firstrider take turns at filling in the grave.

"Somebody who done as much good as Colin should have more than lumps of dirt to mark his place," say Bedelia Coyote. Frank is all for borrowing one of the old tombstones, laying it face-down over Colin, and then writing on the back.

"How're we gonna write on granite?" Rufus wants to know.

"I just use my cock as a jackhammer," say Frank. "One thing I be afraid of though is that I break the stone all apart." That get him punched good by his girlfriend, Connie Bigcharles, and even my girl, Sadie One-wound, take a couple of whacks at him.

We end up taking two white pickets from a fence that be

around an old grave. We drive one in the ground and after looking around for a long time to find something to tie the pickets together to make a cross, Connie Bigcharles take off her panties and we use them to make the cross solid—again the way Colin would of wanted it.

Then Bedelia write on the sideways part of the cross with a felt pen that I carry around for writing down my stories:

Colin Moosefeathers

1954–1979

Gone but not forgotten

Mad Etta, our medicine lady, chant a few prayers and we all head home to get some sleep.

The whole thing started one day up at the Tech School at Wetaskiwin where me and some other guys from the reserve take courses that the government offer on how to be mechanics and stuff. We got to do some physical education too and they divide the students up into four teams for play volleyball, and post the lists in the hall of who is on what team. The team me and Frank are on is have one less player than the others.

"Why don't we add an extra name to even it up?" say Frank. We think for a while and Colin Moosefeathers is about the silliest name we can come up with. It is a white man's funny name mixed with an Indian name that don't mean nothing at all.

I add it at the end of the list. Overnight they must of got the school secretary to retype those lists because next day Colin's name be right there in solid type and in the right alphabetical order just like Colin was a real person.

Every class we go to we have to sign an attendance sheet to show we was there, and I guess it is Donald Bobtail who first sign in Colin Moosefeathers to a diesel-repairing course.

After that one of us is sure to sign him up for every class we attend.

A couple of mornings later we sure surprised to hear over the loudspeaker, in the voice of Mr. McNeil the principal, "Colin Moosefeathers report to the office, please." Us Indian guys have a good laugh and the white students don't pay no attention 'cause to them us Indians all be alike anyway.

"Should we send somebody?" we say to each other. Frank want to go but we figure if they want him to sign anything he be in trouble. Frank is only able to write most of his name and been faking everything else ever since we been here.

Finally, I decide to go. I stick my head in the office, smile at one of the pretty white girls there and say, "You looking for Colin Moosefeathers?"

"Yes," say one who is wearing what look like a man's suit and shoes. "Moosefeathers, we don't have your Social Insurance Number."

"Ain't got one," I say.

The white lady make a cross face. She shove some forms at me. "Here, fill this out and send it in right away. Let me know as soon as you get it. I don't know how they let you in here without one," and she shake her head.

At noon hour we fill it out. We give him Hobbema as an address and 25 as an age. We figure if we make him old then the government won't give him so much hassle. We give Colin my birthday, May 25, but move his birth year back a few from mine. We talk about hanging a second name on him, something like Falling-off-the-roof, but decide not to confuse the government anymore than they already is.

"Any of you guys ever hear of a Colin Moosefeathers?" say Ben Stonebreaker as he is sorting the mail at Hobbema General Store about three weeks later.

"He's my cousin," say Frank.

"Mine too," I say.

"And he's my boyfriend," say Bedelia Coyote.

"Actually, he's my boyfriend and her cousin," say Frank.

"As long as you know him," say Ben. "I don't want the trouble of sending no mail back. Which one of you want his mail?" and boy we pretty well run over each other we is in such a hurry to get outside to see what we got.

What we find is a nice, new Social Insurance card, look just as real as mine, Frank's or Bedelia's.

"What would Colin do with it?" Bedelia say.

Social Insurance ain't good for nothing as far as I can see —only government peoples ever ask for it so they can write down some more numbers to make more work for themselves.

"Bet you could use it to get other things," I say, and the light shine on all three of us about the same time. We get about as excited as when we go looking at used cars on a day when we know somebody has the money to buy one. We go through all the magazines at Blue Quills Hall and all the ones Bedelia Coyote subscribe to, filling out forms for record clubs, book clubs, free postage stamps, even one for a sample strawberry plant. There is one book club where you get a dozen books for a dollar, which is even better than the Buffalo Book Exchange in Edmonton.

But a few weeks go by and we never hear from those places, I guess because we didn't give enough information.

"What if we was to get Colin Moosefeathers a bank account?" I say. "Every form we fill out want to know your bank account number."

Frank and Bedelia jump up and down some and we run to borrow Louis Coyote's pickup truck and head for Wetaskiwin. Along the way we gather up a half-dozen friends and we all troop into the Royal Bank of Canada in Wetaskiwin, laughing and pushing each other.

The tellers all try to look busy so we have to go to some

other stall but finally one of them have to let her white customer go and we walk up to the counter. "Can I help you?" she say, wrinkling her nose.

"I want to open up an account," I say, and slap down Colin's Social Insurance card to prove that I am a real person.

"How much do you want to deposit?" say the lady.

"How much do I have to?" I ask.

"You have to deposit at least one dollar, Mr. Moosefeathers," the lady say, while everyone behind me laugh and jump around. We get a quarter each from four people and open the account after taking about ten minutes to decide what kind of account it should be. There must be 50 different types that pay interest or don't and what I can write cheques on or can't.

"All I want is an account number for a form I got to fill out," I say to the teller lady who have blue glasses and what look like a hearing aid in her ear. But she still make me pick and choose and I end up with something like a personal chequing account what I can write fifteen cheques on and still get interest. Seem like a lot of choosing to have to do for a dollar. But when we finally leave Colin Moosefeathers have his very own bank account.

"Now what?" say my girlfriend Sadie.

"Let's write some cheques," say Frank. "We is rich Indians."

But it is Winnie Bear who do the important thing in the bank. She picked up application forms for Mastercard and Visa cards.

Before, when we send away to record clubs, and for strawberry plants and cuckoo clocks we usually just leave the occupation and income lines blank. On one form Frank have me put down his occupation as an Indian.

"It's a full-time job being one," he say, but it don't get him no records either.

Winnie Bear also dig out from her purse a ratty-looking credit card application from the Hobbema Texaco Garage. "What if we were to send this in for Colin? A guy with a brand new Social Insurance Number and a bank account shouldn't have to sell pop bottles to buy gas."

Me and Bedelia fill out the form. We put the Social Insurance Number right across the top in red pen. We argue for a long time about occupation before we put down Indian Agent, and we give Colin a wife, two kids, a 1975 Oldsmobile car, a mobile home and $15,000 in the spot on the form ask for income.

We have to pool up our money to buy stamps for the letters that don't have paid postage on them. By the end of the day Colin Moosefeathers has applied for credit from Mastercard, Visa, Simpsons-Sears Department Store, Esso, Texaco, Gulf, Pacific 66, and we filled out every form we can find in all the back issues of *Weekend*, *Saturday Night*, *Time*, *Newsweek* and the *Western Producer*, and whatever other magazines we can locate at the Wetaskiwin public library. I'm even feeling so good I pay my 10¢ and get Colin a library card of his own, even though I already have one in my name.

We check with Ben Stonebreaker every day to see if Colin got any mail but a month or so goes by and nothing come. We start to get sad again and some days we even forget to check. Then the letters start coming in a rush. They mostly say the same thing, "Sorry, but we can't give you no credit," but then a brand new Mastercard, all shiny and smell like the kitchenware section at Robinson's Stores, arrive. I sign, *Colin Moosefeathers*, on the white space on the back and then we just all sit around and look at it laying on the table. It is a white card with overlapping circles of red and gold, a fourteen-figure number across the middle, and printed neat as you please at the bottom is COLIN MOOSEFEATHERS, and an expiry date for three months from now.

We was kind of shy with it at first, sort of like being with a white girl in a dress, not knowing what to say, where, or if to touch.

I went into Robinson's Store in Wetaskiwin and picked out a black felt hat with a cherry-coloured headband, and a bluish-green feather that stick clear up over the top. On the way to the cashier I grab two lipsticks, one called *Love's Fresh Raspberry* is for Sadie, and the other one called *Love's Ghostly Lips*, be white, and I get it for Connie Bigcharles 'cause she like to smear that kind of stuff on her face.

I look at the cashier lady and she look back at me. I'm waiting for her to ask, "Is this cash or charge?" like she done to the three people in front of me.

"Well?" she say to me. I guess she never expect an Indian to have a Mastercard.

I pull out the card and lay it on the counter. The saleslady look at me and the card two or three times. When she read it and see the name is Indian just like me, she take out from under the counter a long list of credit card numbers and check close to be sure Colin's card ain't on it.

"Ain't never used it before," I say as I sign Colin's name and show her the other identification I got in what I call Colin's wallet, a 99¢ holder I bought right after the Social Insurance card come.

Boy, everybody is sure excited when I get back to the street. "It was easy," I tell them. We all talk at once. Everybody want something different; it is like finding a wallet full of lots and lots of money.

"Guitar,"

"Clothes,"

"Car,"

"Booze,"

"Stereo set," everybody is making their requests.

"It's like kidnapping Santa Claus," say Winnie Bear.

"Let's everybody make a list," I say. "Then we'll go and buy all the stuff as quick as we can before this here company change its mind."

We find out a couple of things right away, for one we can't buy nothing that cost more than $100 without the store phoning somewhere to see if it is okay. And we find out too that we ain't allowed to buy more than a $500 total.

"We have to buy small and fast," I say.

Frank is disappointed when he find out he can't buy a car, and that the Alberta Government Liquor Store don't take Mastercard. It ain't even good at the Alice Hotel beer parlour. The Travelodge Restaurant is okay, and we all have steaks and bottled beer for lunch.

Connie and Sadie buy sweaters, rings, scarves and a lot of makeup. We buy guitars, leather jackets, a new drum for Rufus, some books and a butterfly in a box for Winnie Bear. Bedelia buy hiking boots and three pairs of jeans. Frank get a big black hat like mine and an electric can-opener. At Cunningham Drugs we buy up about ten cartons of cigarettes and lots of after-shave, perfume and deodorant in spray cans.

Then we remember our people at home. I buy for my Ma and brothers and sisters and I even buy from the Tip Top Men's Wear Store one of them funny little hats with no brim to send to my brother-in-law in Calgary. From the pet store I get a guinea pig in a cage for my brother Joseph. We think good things about Mad Etta too. We go to the Big and Tall Shop in Wetaskiwin but the largest dress there wouldn't cover but half of Mad Etta. We do buy her the biggest one they got which be size 54 and of a colour that look like somebody crammed a rainbow in a washtub and stirred. We then go to Wetaskiwin Tent and Awning and buy up ten yards of what the man call sailcloth what is cov-

ered in a big white daisy pattern. We talk about taking it to
the Singer Sewing Machine Company and telling them to
sew it up into a dress, but we too shy for that and they might
think we was joking anyway.

Then we remember Louis Coyote's pickup truck. We already filled it up with gas, oil, STP and anti-freeze. But then
we remember that the tires be thin and bald as old men.

"Mag wheels," somebody shout, and we head for Fire-
stone Tire Co. Them wheels cost a lot more than we figure
so we only buy one, then we go to a service station and buy
a radial tire for it. Truck sure look funny with one shiny
silver wheel and one ordinary one, but by going to different
stores we get it all decked out in radial tires and mag wheels.
Then we price a paint job: truck at one time was a dark blue
colour but lately it ain't much of anything. Paint-job man
wants $200 for his cheapest work—we can't afford to get it
candy-appled the way we would all like. "Can we get it done
half one day and half the next," we ask. He is hungry for
business so he agree to put the charge on two tickets so he
don't have to phone us in to the company.

That is something we found out: people is real greedy
and will take a chance if it gonna mean a sale for them. Like
when we decided to buy a sofa to sit up in the back of the
truck so we can seat Mad Etta there when we want to haul
her someplace and not have to carry out her tree-trunk chair
every time.

The man at Honest Lou's Furniture Discount Store and
RV Centre, phone in Colin's credit card number and get told
he can't charge the $495 for the sofa 'cause we already gone
over the limit. "Mastercard says maybe I should pick up the
card from you. They suspect it's being misused," he say.

"Oh no," we say. "We just buying this here sofa for our
sick mother." So that salesman write up five coffee tables at
$99 and put each one on a separate ticket.

"What they don't know won't hurt them," he say to us and we all agree with him.

We live like white people for about a week. Then the phone calls start coming. Fred Crier at the Texaco Garage and Ben Stonebreaker at the General Store both say somebody been phoning and asking for Colin Moosefeathers and I bet if we was to ask at the school or the Department of Indian Affairs Office why they been phoning there too. They leave urgent messages for Colin to call numbers in Edmonton and even Montreal.

Some guy from Indian Affairs come stepping around on soft-soled shoes, walk sideways like a coyote, want to know who Colin is and how come he claimed to be an Indian Agent? Indian Affairs guys are all real pale 'cause they stay in their office buildings all the time. I guess they all from the city someplace and only know about paper Indians from books and is afraid of the real kind like us.

"Finance men!" one of the kids yell next morning as he run into Ben Stonebreaker's store. Me and Frank and Rufus run fast for the culvert and we barely get it pulled out of the road when a new, dark blue Dodge skid to a stop almost putting its front wheels in the hole in the road. Four guys in suits, vests and hats get out, one from each door, look like FBI agents we seen on the television.

"Sorry about the road," we say. "Cabins is a mile or so up the hill. You have to walk if you want to get there."

"Last white man who went up there was never heard from again," say Frank.

"Just tell us where we can find Colin Moosefeathers," say the driver.

"Colin's dead," I say, thinking real fast.

"When?" say another finance man, taking out a black notebook and a fountain pen.

"Week ago," I say.

"Two weeks," say Rufus.

"How?"

"Drowned," I say.

"Fire," say Rufus.

"Fist fight," say Frank.

"He's buried at the graveyard," I say, pointing up the hill. "Only a two-mile walk. We'll take you." We know that white men don't like to walk more than a few feet at a time so we're pretty sure they won't take us up on it and they don't.

They go away but claim they going to the RCMP to find out how and when Colin died, and that is about the last thing we want them to.

We have us a meeting that afternoon and decide it be a good idea if we was really to kill off Colin Moosefeathers. We make a couple of last buys like a wreath of plastic flowers for his grave, and then we go stand around the Alberta Government Liquor Store until we spot a man dressed in a suit and tie . . . those kind be the most anxious to make quick money maybe because they all the time have to pay for expensive clothes.

"Hey, Mister," we say. "You buy us $50 worth of liquor and we let you charge $100 on our Mastercard." The guy look all around, like a dog gonna steal food off the table, then nod his head. We have to let him do his charging first but he is a little afraid of us and he buy what we want.

We set the credit card in the middle of the table at Big-charles' cabin and that is where we have the all-night party, kind of a wake, before we do the burying in the early morning.

That afternoon the RCMP come rolling in, a whole car-load of them, led by Constable Chretien, who is about the dumbest RCMP there ever was.

"We have a report of a suspicious death," say Constable

Chretien, who speak English with a French accent as thick as ours is Cree. He write down everything we tell him, and we tell him different every time he ask. The other constables, who be fuzzy-cheeked as Mormon Missionaries, even get to laughing after a while, but Constable Chretien take everything personally.

My mouth is dry as a brown paper bag from talking so much. We finally take the constables up to the graveyard and show them Colin Moosefeathers' grave, with the cross over it and the plastic flowers on it, while Constable Chretien give us a lecture on how deaths have to be reported to a doctor and the coroner and the RCMP and maybe even to the government in Edmonton too.

Bedelia give him a big argument on how we reported the death to Mad Etta, who be our doctor, and how the government said that is all we have to do, and hasn't he read the directive from Ottawa on it. . . . Bedelia be so good at arguing with police and government people that she just about convince me that she is right, except I can tell she's making it up as she goes along when she say that the directive come from the Department of Ashcans and Propaganda. The young RCMPs all laugh but Constable Chretien stay serious because he is a page or two behind in his writing down what Bedelia says, and don't even hear the funny part.

"We will have to exhume the body," he says.

We all argue loud about that but Constable Chretien radio to Wetaskiwin and out come the coroner, a doctor and a couple of guys with shovels, all ride in a shiny white ambulance. About half the reserve is stand around that evening while the guys dig up the grave. As they getting to the bottom and not finding anything Bedelia pipe up, "Guess we forgot to tell you that we cremated him," and everybody have a big laugh. Some kids brought out their portable radio, tuned to CKWX in Camrose and some of us dance to the country songs they is playing. Some other people make a campfire and kids is cooking wieners and marshmallows.

They get to the bottom without even finding the credit card which we cut up in about a dozen pieces with Eathen Firstrider's hunting knife.

"This grave is empty," say Constable Chretien, and everyone give a big cheer.

"Hey partner," Bedelia say to him. "You shouldn't look so surprised. It's happened before. You must of read about it," and everybody cheer again. Constable Chretien look disgusted. "Don't be mad," Bedelia go on. "We might be in right at the start of something for all we know."

THE RUNNER

At the Commonwealth Games in Edmonton last summer one of the guys who didn't win any medals was Mark Antelope. Not only he don't win, but in the last race he run he broke what they call the Achilles bone in his foot so he never be able to foot-race no more. Mark become eighteen just a few days before that happen.

I never knew him good until he come home 'cause he ain't lived on the reserve since he was about seven years old. That year a bunch of people from Canada Sports—or maybe with the way the government turn all the names around to make them French, it was Sports Canada—come around the reserve, have all the boys and girls at the reserve school do running, tumbling, high jump and stuff like that. The government people look like teachers wearing red sweat-suits: the men have thick waists and slap everybody on the back, the women have thin faces and smell of peppermint.

Most of us kids don't bother doing none of that running or jumping for them, but the little kids don't know no better and some of them, like Mark Antelope and Debbie Birdshot, catch their eye. My friend Frank Fence-post ask if they got an event for snatch and grab five-finger bargains from stores, 'cause that be the one he'd like to sign up for. He don't get an answer, just some dark-coloured looks.

Debbie was able to jump the same as her height and the sweatsuits say she be real good if she was to get some training. And they like Mark too. He was maybe three years younger than me but could run away from me like I was standing still. The sweatsuit people go to the families of those kids they like, say how if they let their kids move off to Edmonton for now and maybe Ottawa later, they get school and good training for sports. To the parents it seem like a good idea especially since they ain't being asked to pay for it, and to the kids it look like a lot of fun.

After that, Mark only come home for a week twice a year. After the first year or so Debbie Birdshot stopped coming altogether and I heard that she been adopted by some white people off in the East and don't even be an Indian no more.

After his accident, Sports Canada they just pack up Mark's things and give him his bus fare back to Hobbema.

"I don't know what to do with myself," he say. "I know what an old man must feel like after he worked all his life and then gets retired. Running was a job for me. I like to try and get me a regular job but it don't count much to put on an application that you run the 1500 metres for a living for ten years."

Mark been on the Canada Running Team since he was fourteen and he travelled all over the world to run in races, and he win a lot. We seen his face come on TV one night in the bar of the Alice Hotel in Wetaskiwin. We yell everybody down and get the bartender to turn up the sound. This here TV announcer, Ernie Afaganis, was doing a story about Mark Antelope. Ernie Afaganis, I guess, is what a sport announcer is supposed to look like: he is always so washed and dressed and pretty only way you know it is really him and not a photograph is that his lips move a little. On the TV they show pictures of Mark before a race against guys from Africa, Australia, Germany and faraway places like that, and they show too how before every race he shake hands with the other runners and give to them a little wooden tomahawk, have the Canadian flag glued to one side of it. Mark is slim and light brown coloured, have wide-spaced dark eyes and his short hair shine blue-black in the TV light.

He still wear his hair short. We wish he would grow braids like me and Rufus Firstrider, or else leave his hair long and wild like Frank.

"Just a few more years and I could have been a coach. If not for the track team then for a high school somewhere," Mark say.

"Why couldn't you do that anyway?" I ask.

"See, all through school there was always somebody there to help me, a tutor they're called. I was always away on trips to run in track meets or off to someplace special to practise. I never went to regular school and I think lots of times the tutor put in marks a lot better than I should of got. According to them I have only half a year left to finish my grade twelve, but when I went into the grade twelve class here, I couldn't read good, or understand the work. Only thing I know how to do is run. If I want to go to university now, I got to make it on my own. And you know how tough that be."

I sure do. I only know one or two people in all my life from the reserve that got to university. I try to think of something kind to say to Mark. When I put myself in his place it seem to me that it must be awful scary.

"It hard for me to be Indian," Mark go on. "I feel like I'm spoiled. . . ."

"You was born an Indian," I say. "You hang around with us guys for a while and you get back in the swing of things."

Mark say he'd like to do something Indian like trapping or hunting, so we ask Robert Striker to take him out on his trapline with him. We fix Mark up with a parka, some moccasins and leggings. They be gone for a couple of weeks only, and Robert Striker come back shaking his head.

"That guy don't know enough to come in out of the cold," he say. "He can't shoot a rifle, or skin an ermine and he let the fire go out at night. . . ."

"How you figure you'd get along your first time on a city job?" we ask Robert, but he just say he don't want Mark with him no more.

Bedelia Coyote take a kind of liking to Mark. She is only a year or so older than him and don't usually like men. She believe in this here Women's Rights stuff and always fight with the government over something.

"Maybe if we asked Chief Tom he could get Mark a government job," we suggest.

"Don't count on it," say Bedelia. But we all know that if he wanted to, Chief Tom could arrange a scholarship to the university or to the Tech School in Wetaskiwin. If my friend Frank Fence-post could get into the Tech School anybody should be able to.

Chief Tom is dumb as a sackful of hammers, which I guess make him able to get along easy with the other elected guys in the government. Besides be our Chief here on the Ermineskin Reserve, he last year run for MLA as a Conservative, and he win easy. In Alberta all you got to do is sign up your name with Premier Lougheed and you get elected.

First thing Chief Tom done after he got elected is hire his girlfriend, Samantha Yellowknees, as his Executive Assistant, for what Bedelia Coyote say is $22,500 a year. Chief Tom left his wife on the reserve a couple of years ago and him and Samantha live in an apartment in Wetaskiwin got a sauna bath, and a talk-back machine at the front door.

The government be in session so we have to go all the way to Edmonton to find Chief Tom. Him and Samantha be holed up in the Chateau Lacombe Hotel, a fancy place that have thick carpets and smell like the inside of a new car. We borrow Louis Coyote's pickup truck and me, Frank Fence-post, his girlfriend Connie Bigcharles, Mark, Bedelia, Rufus Firstrider and his white girlfriend Winnie Bear, go off to Edmonton.

I guess the lady on the desk, who wear a red jacket and look like she never seen Indians before, must of phoned the room, because Samantha meet us in the hall. She have her hair tied tight in a bun, wear a lemon-coloured dress and hold tight to her chest a clipboard where she write out notes for Chief Tom. Samantha come from Ontario and been to a university someplace. If it wasn't for her, Chief Tom still be cutting brush for the railway.

Chief Crow-eye is too busy to see us, is what she tell us, but if we tell her the problem she'll tell him. While she is saying this, Frank, Connie and Bedelia walk right into the room. Eventually we all get there, Samantha backing up every step of the way and arguing.

Chief Tom wearing a blue velvet robe and eating bacon and eggs off a tray.

"Well, young people," he say, "come in, come in. What can I do for you today?" While he is saying this he look hard at Samantha as if to say, "How did these guys ever get in here?"

Bedelia introduce him to Mark and Mark present him with one of them little wooden tomahawks got the Canadian flag on it. Then Bedelia talk to Chief Tom in Cree, which we all know embarrass him, 'cause he like to pretend that he's not really an Indian no more.

"On behalf of the Government of Alberta, and the constituency of Wetaskiwin and the Ermineskin Reserve, I want to welcome you," Chief Tom say to Mark. Samantha rush over to Chief Tom and whisper to him from some notes she just made on her clipboard, and he smile and go on to tell

99

Mark what a great runner he was and how everybody, and he name them all again, is real proud of him.

Then Bedelia get right down to what we came for, ask about a job or free school for Mark. Mark, he talk a little in English say he'd sure like some help to get his life started again.

Chief Tom, he sympathize with Mark about his injury for a long time but he also slip in how there ain't very many jobs around and how he is only a small cog in the big machine of government.

"How come you was able to find Samantha here a good job?" Bedelia want to know, and that make Chief Tom go into another speech for ten minutes or so that don't even come close to answering the question.

While they are talking, Frank, he get on the telephone to this place called Room Service. Him and me learned all about that one time when we was in a big hotel in the United States.

"This here's Chief Tom Crow-eye's room," he say into the phone. "You send up seven tequila sunrises . . . doubles . . . and a couple of cases of Lethbridge Pale Ale, some ham and tomato sandwiches . . . toasted, with pickles, and make them three-deckers, some potato chips, and Cheesies, and you got any Chinese food? No. Well, a few hamburgers then, and chocolate bars . . ."

"And bubble gum," say Connie into his ear. So he order some of that too.

"And a couple of cartons of Export A cigarettes, and say, do you guys got clothes down there too or just food?" When he find out he can't get shirts or shoes, he settle for the stuff he already ordered. "And you charge that up to the Honourable Member from Wetaskiwin," and he hang up and smile big.

Samantha Yellowknees read off some notes from her clipboard, ask Mark to talk about himself and how he come to get hurt. "It was the race for the gold medal and I was closing in on these two guys from Kenya. It happened just as I was going into my final kick, like shift a car into overdrive, that I bust my foot. I have to pull up and in a couple of seconds even the slowest runner has gone by me, the race is over and everybody is hugging everybody else way down at the finish line and there I am sitting on the edge of the track way around at the final turn waiting for the trainers to come and get me."

I remember another time, me and Mark was sitting in the beer parlour of the Alice Hotel in Wetaskiwin. I took him up there figuring that if he had a few beers he'd feel a little happier, but Mark never been allowed beer before and he don't like it. I coax him into a couple anyway and get him to talking. "I realize I can't ever race no more. But what hurt worse is that I claim all these years to be an Indian but I'm not really. I don't speak the language no more. My folks are strange to me. We try to be nice to each other but there's nothing there. Everything smells bad to me. You smell bad to me, Silas, your clothes stink of wood smoke. Ma feeds me good, but the plates are greasy and the food I used to like as a kid makes me sick."

That night he tell me, too, of his dream of running a victory lap around that Commonwealth Games track in Edmonton waving to them 40,000 peoples who would be standing up and cheering him, and how he say that since he know he never do that, he have dreams of running across the top of the High Level Bridge in Edmonton, carrying a torch like they do for the Olympic Games. He say he have that dream almost every night.

We all tried to make Mark feel at home, but he don't like to party much and he always end up going off by himself.

After Chief Tom hear Mark's story, he stand himself up

to his full size, which come to about Mark's shoulder, smile at him and wish him best of luck on behalf of everybody again. "Young fellow," he say, "I know that your spirit and strong heart will carry you through. Always remember that when the going gets tough, the tough get going."

"I told you all he'd get from Chief Tom was advice," I whisper to Bedelia. She is so mad she stomp her foot on the floor and head for the door. The rest of us follow, except Frank who is still waiting for his order to come. "Have a nice day, young people," Chief Tom is saying from the doorway, already he is starting a big sigh as he close the door. Then around the corner come a bellboy in a blue uniform push a cart loaded with all the stuff Frank ordered.

"Hey, we decide to move the party to another place," say Frank.

"The parking-lot," say Winnie Bear, and everybody laugh.

"We just take this stuff along with us," we say and start to load up our hands. That bellboy don't know whether to let us or not, but there is seven of us and me, Frank and Rufus is pretty tough-looking dudes.

"You just take the bill to the door there. Chief Tom will sign and give you a tip," and boy do we ever clear out of there fast, drinking our tequila sunrises, what was Winnie Bear's idea to order, as we go.

As kind of a last try we figure that if we get Mark a woman that sure help to make him feel at home again. Like I said, Bedelia got her eyes on Mark but he don't seem to like her back. Anyway, Bedelia ain't much for pretty and she act strict as a schoolteacher a lot of the time. We fix him up with Cindy Claw. Nobody know for sure who her father was, but he likely was white. She is long-legged and delicate as the tiger-lilies that grow out on the hills. She so pretty she make me smile to think of her, and I always take a short breath when she walk into a room.

"You like Mark Antelope?" we come right out and ask her one afternoon.

"He's the best looking guy I've seen for a long time. All the girls go for him," she say. "But he never pay no attention to us."

"Well, he likes you," we tell Cindy, "only he's too shy to say so."

That night at the dance at Blue Quills Hall, Cindy, she hang herself all over Mark like he was a chair and she was some empty clothes. It ain't hard to see what Cindy got in mind and pretty early in the evening they leave the hall with arms around each other's waists.

It is only an hour or so before Cindy is back and it easy to see that she's not very happy. "What kind of crazy guy is he anyway?" Cindy yell at me and Frank.

"What did he do?" we want to know.

"He didn't do nothing. That's what he did. He act like I make him sick and he give me one of these," and she throw at my face one of the wooden tomahawks. "Then he go walking off talking to himself."

Late that night as I'm walking up the hill from the dance hall I meet Mark coming down. He try at first to pretend he don't see me.

"You going someplace?" I ask. I can see he's carrying his duffel bag, a red one with a white maple leaf on it.

"Someplace," he say.

"Did something bad happen with Cindy? We was just trying to get you a friend, make you feel at home here."

"I know. It's me, Silas. I been with white girls, it's just that with Indian girls I can't."

I look at him in the moonlight, his face is smooth as the brown wax paper you see in butcher shops, his eyes look like they is about to flood. Mark swing his duffel bag up on his back. "I ain't Indian no more," he say. "Maybe you could understand, Silas. You could never be white. The old ways stick to you like burrs to a wool sock."

I want to say to him that he can't ever be white either, but I don't.

"I'm no more Indian than those little tomahawks I hand out. If you look close you see they was made over in Korea."

He take down the bag from his shoulder, open it up and hand to me a box full of his tomahawks. "Give them to your little brothers and sisters," he say. And then, "Silas, if you ever come to Edmonton and some night you see a man in a track suit running across the top deck of the High Level bridge, carrying a torch in his hand, or maybe just hold up an empty hand in pretending, you know who it is you seeing up there."

He swing on past me down the road and for a while I can see the white maple leaf on his duffel bag until it get too dark even for that.

YELLOW SCARF

In memory of Susan Glaspell

"Bring your ma along, Silas," Mad Etta say to me from the back window of the RCMP car. "I feel better if I got another woman along on a bad business like this."

Corporal Greer is driving and a young constable sit beside him. There is a guy in a business suit and an overcoat drive a white government car and follow along behind the police car.

Ma been hoping she would get asked. She already got on her good purple dress and last night she steamed the spots from her red winter coat and sewed up the lining.

Mad Etta is sit up there in the back of the police car, her head like a big round pumpkin that sit on top of a pup tent like they got in the window of Wetaskiwin Tent and Awning. Take five flour sacks to make Mad Etta a dress and she weigh so much that the springs of the police car be pushed down just about as far as they can go. Mad Etta be the medicine lady for our tribe, but this ain't no doctoring call we is going on.

"Marcel, you go ride with the coroner in the other car," Corporal Greer say to the young guy. "Silas, you and Mrs. Ermineskin sit up here with me."

It is one of those March days when the wind chews at everything, and even though the sun is shine some it is far away and no good for anything but light things up.

"Mrs. Crier wants Etta to pick up a few things for her from the house, and Silas, I don't want you to be worried, all you have to do is tell me and the coroner exactly what you found when you went to Crier's place yesterday," say Corporal Greer.

The Crier place is about two miles back in the bush. It sits down in a hollow off to the right of the road. It is about the only two-storey house on the reserve, and ain't never been painted. As we come down the hill toward it, there be a few poplars, look all silvery and cold as the March snow, and some short red willow, bare and shiny. A few tufts of meadow grass show through the snow.

There is a corral all trampled up black from the last thaw, but frozen solid this morning. There be a couple of gaunt red-and-white steers stand in the far corner, their backs set against the wind.

Both cars turn into the yard, pull up in front of the house and we get out.

"This is Dr. Leopold, coroner for the County of Wetaskiwin," say Corporal Greer. We shake hands. The coroner is wearing leather gloves.

It take all three of us quite a while to get Mad Etta out of the back of that car. Usually we haul Etta around in the back of Louis Coyote's pickup truck. We put her tree-trunk chair up there for her to sit on and in winter we cover her up with a tarpaulin.

"Hope you never get drunk and sassy, Etta," say Corporal Greer. "Sure hate to have to try and get you in and out of there if you weren't co-operating with us." Etta, she laugh and laugh, and wheeze some, like she just run a mile or so.

Corporal Greer is a pretty good guy for an RCMP. He

must be gonna retire soon. His face is about as grey as his hair, and he got sad pouches under his eyes like a dog.

There are a couple of slab sheds in the yard, two wrecked cars, a 1960 Dodge pickup that I seen Martin Crier drive in the summer. Off to the left of the house there is half a combine sinking into the ground. Near the front door is a cream can painted the pale blue colour of the Northern Alberta Dairy Pool, and an upside-down washtub, both pretty rusty. I can hear a chicken but I can't decide where it's at.

"I'm glad you come with me, Suzie," Mad Etta say to Ma as we follow the police and coroner into the house. It sure sound funny to hear somebody call Ma by her first name.

Inside, the house smell like sour milk. There is a drop-leaf table with one leaf down and pushed against the wall under the window. The outside leaf been broken off and the hinges hang down looking greasy. There is last year's flies on the windowsill and the window be real dirty. A Vogue tobacco tin holds a spindly geranium that is all stalk and no flower. It is kind of black-looking from been frozen. The house is cold and we can see our breath puff out like maybe all of us was smoking, but only Mad Etta got a cigarette going.

There is an oil-drum stove with the stove pipes run straight up through the ceiling. A *Roger's Golden Syrup* can full of water and a black frying pan sit on the stove. A rocking-chair with half the spokes busted out of the back sit off to one side, and two kitchen chairs, one with the back gone, is the rest of the furniture. There is a narrow little cupboard against the back wall with some pans and dishes on it, a washbasin and a pail of drinking water. A slop pail sit on the floor.

In the corner is a big pile of stuff: harness and rags, a five-gallon jerry can, bits of lumber, and a broke-up chain-saw is some of the things I can see.

The one thing that sure strikes me is that there is no colour anyplace. This sure ain't a very happy place to be.

"Were you a friend of Mrs. Crier's?" Corporal Greer say to Ma.

"I knew her good when we was young, but not so good lately. I ain't been down here to see her for a long time. She stopped going out a few years ago, and her Mister wasn't one to like people around."

Corporal Greer don't say anything so Ma figures she should talk some more.

"Lots of times I said to myself I should go down and see Helen, but there was always something to do, what with all my kids around . . ."

To me it is kind of funny how good Ma can talk English when something serious going on. Lots of times I seen her pretend to Corporal Greer that she don't speak or understand nothing but Cree.

Corporal Greer shiver a little, clap his hands together and say to me, "Silas, I want you to tell Dr. Leopold and me what you found when you were here yesterday." When he say that his voice is different from before and he talk like a police officer.

That coroner fellow is walk around the room like maybe he gonna get his feet dirty. "Filth, filth," he be muttering under his breath. Out loud he say, "Have things been moved around since yesterday?"

Corporal Greer look around the room real careful, then look over to Constable Marcel who nods. "Everything is the same," he say. Then he nod to me. Both him and the coroner got out black notebooks to write down what I say.

"I walked out here yesterday," I say, my voice breaking a bit on the word yesterday. Corporal Greer nod and give me a little smile that say I should go on. "I got the job to make up the voter's list for the next election. I know most everyone on the reserve but the forms say I got to visit everyone personal. That was why I come down, 'cause I'm the enum ... enum ..."

"Enumerator," say Dr. Leopold, impatient like.

"I walk up to the door and knock. It was all quiet inside the house. Nobody answered so I knocked again real loud. Nobody said anything but I heard something move so I open the door and there was Mrs. Crier sit in the rocking-chair."

Everybody is look at the rocking-chair some.

"What did she look like?" say the coroner.

"She don't look good."

"What do you mean by that?"

I not sure how to explain it to him. I haven't seen Mrs. Crier very many times, but I heard people talk about her. They say she be as pretty at one time as my sister Illianna, but there ain't nothing pretty about her now. Her face is long and sad and her hair is straight and ain't been combed for a while. That house smell sour, and that is the way she look, sour. She is really thin, a kind of yellow colour, and the joints of her fingers look like they swollen up.

"Well she just looked strange. She smiled kind of sad at me and was humming under her breath."

"She used to sing in the choir at the Residential School," say Ma. "Had a voice as sweet as a robin."

The coroner look harsh at Ma and she shut up. Guess he don't want to know about things like that.

"How did she react to you? Was she glad to see you?"

"She don't seem to care much. I said, 'Hello, Mrs. Crier. I'm Silas Ermineskin, come to get your name on the voters' list.' She don't answer me, just sit and twist her scarf in her fingers."

"Scarf?"

"A grey speckled one, like a lot of Indian ladies wear on their hair."

"What then?"

"She look to me like maybe she is sick or something, so I figure I better talk to her husband. 'Can I see Mr. Crier?' 'No,' she say to me in a kind of sleepy way. 'Is he home?' I ask her. I don't want to be a bother to her but the nearest farm to this is over a mile and I don't want to have to make another trip out here.

"Then she look up at me for the first time. 'He's home,' she say and go back to twisting up her scarf."

The coroner is tapping his foot and making notes real fast like he would like me to hurry with my story, but I want to be real careful of what I tell him. Like he wouldn't be interested in my tell him about the look in her eyes when she first look at me, just for a second it was there, then her eyes be dark and blank like mud puddles.

"I start to ask again if I can see him, but Mrs. Crier cut me off by saying, 'He's dead.' She say it casual like she was saying it's cold outside, or have some tea.

"I repeat that word, dead, to be sure I heard right. She just look at me and rock some in that chair there. Then she just point to the upstairs with her bony hand, but she don't look up there at all.

" 'What happened to him?' I ask.

" 'He died of a knife stuck in his neck,' she say in barely a whisper, and go on twisting her scarf all up.

"Couple of times I start to go upstairs have a look, but it is just so quiet out here and the wind is whistle under the door and squeak in the corners of the window. It is cold too, I think she already let the stove go out.

" 'Who done it?' I ask, taking a deep breath.

"She shrug her shoulders some.

" 'Weren't you here when it happened?'

" 'I was sleeping,' she say, as if that is all there is to it.

" 'You called the RCMP?' I say. I don't figure she has,

but I figure I should ask anyway.

" 'You do that for me . . .' and she pause a long time 'cause she already forgot my name."

"What did you do then, Silas?" say Corporal Greer.

"I run all the way to Hobbema Crossing to the store and phone you guys."

"Okay, Silas, thank you. We'll go upstairs now, Dr. Leopold. Marcel . . . Constable Prefontaine, was the one who answered the call. He can tell you about finding the body."

"Young man," say the coroner. "Do you think she was telling the truth about sleeping while someone came in and murdered her husband?"

I take a long time before I answer him, like I thinking about it real careful, then all I say is, "Yes." I would like to maybe yell at him, "Little skinny lady like that, be maybe 45, look at least 65, you think she gonna kill a big, fat Indian like Martin Crier. He could squeeze her to death with just one hand if he wanted to," but I don't say or do nothing except look at the floor some.

"She's a cool one, if you ask me," say Constable Marcel. "She gave me the same story about how she slept. . . . He was killed from his side of the bed, and whoever did it held the knife in the sheet. We dusted it for prints but there were none."

The coroner look at Corporal Greer. "You certain that there's nothing important down here? Don't want these people touching anything they aren't supposed to touch."

"Marcel and I had a good look around yesterday. Nothing here that would point to a motive. Just this junk," and he wave his hand to show that everything around be junk, and he laugh a little then to show the coroner that he don't have to worry none about leave us Indians alone. They go upstairs.

"Do you think she done it?" Ma say to Mad Etta. Etta roll her eyes some. "Etta don't know. Them Mounties think she did."

"Well, I don't," say Ma. "You know why? You say she asked for you to bring her scarves that she been sewing up, and for that house plant of hers. Now if I'd just killed somebody, and there was plenty of times when I thought of kill that no-good husband of mine, I wouldn't be worrying about no plants."

"That plant is too bad froze to take anywhere," I say.

"Them kind got strong roots," say Mad Etta.

We can hear them walk around upstairs, make the floor squeak.

"It is kind of funny that a woman be charged with murder worry about her plant," say Etta. "But that coroner guy he gonna make it hard for her if he get the chance, so is the young constable. They make fun that she could sleep while someone come in and kill Martin."

"Well it don't look like he woke up when he got stabbed," Ma persist. "Not like her to keep so bad a house. She used to take the home economics at school and be really good at it. Sew as good as anybody and cook lots of fancy things. But look at that stove, don't suppose there are more than a couple of oil-drum stoves left on the reserve. I guess I'd kind of give up too if I had so little to work with."

About all I know about Martin Crier is that he worked sometimes in the summer, cut brush off the right-of-ways for the railroad. He got a big beer-belly and be so mean that hardly anybody ever pick a fight with him. He used to spend a lot of time in the Alice Hotel beer parlour, and guess he drink quite a bit around home too by the number of empties there be around the house and yard.

"I went to school for a lot of years with Helen Bobtail," Ma say. "I always think of her as Helen Bobtail even if she been Helen Crier for what must be close to twenty years.

"She used to dance when she was a girl. Used to stomp

around the Blue Quills Hall or up at the hall at Bittern Lake, used to have dances up there on Friday nights. Helen Bobtail would wear a yellow scarf in her hair, and it trailed out behind her when she danced. We used to tease her some, say if she had an old-time Indian name it be Yellow Scarf. Used to say too, maybe she wished she had yellow hair like the white girls at the dances.

"She was kind of wild in those days, but no worse than the rest of us I guess. Then she married with Martin Crier. He was a handsome man, big-chested and wear his hair in two braids, but solemn like cold water. I never seen him dance."

"Martin Crier was cold as the weather today," say Etta. "Hardly knew either one of them, but I was out here once, five or six years ago. Helen came for me, said Martin had a bad chest. I put herb plasters on him and give him a big shot of whisky. Even then Helen look worse than some that's got ten to twelve kids. I didn't ask for no money from them but Martin Crier pulled a twenty out of his pocket. 'I pay my way,' he said. And them was the only words he spoke to me."

"I wish you could of seen Helen Bobtail in her white dress and with a yellow scarf tied in her hair when she graduate from the Residential School." say Ma.

I look around some while they is talk. On the cupboard there is two cracked mugs with dry tea bags in them. There is a can of beans, been opened but never poured nowhere, and a slab of bacon been set on the cupboard and got one slice taken off it. Look to me like Helen Crier was making a meal, and then stopped for something and never started up again. I sure wonder what that could be.

"It don't seem right that they come sneak around Helen's house after they lock her up," say Ma.

"If she ain't done it, I suppose they find that out too," say Etta.

Way at the back of the counter is a half full can of cat food with a spoon sticking in it. On the floor beside the stove is a saucer with some dried-up cat food that smell pretty ripe. I wonder if maybe she took the cat with her to jail.

"How'd you like to live in a place like this, Etta?" say Ma. "You think this belong to a bum like Fred Bottle or that they got maybe fifteen kids instead of none. Martin hold a job quite often and don't be as bad a drinker as my old man but they got nothing. What do you figure Martin Crier done with his money?"

Instead of answer Etta talk about something else.

"She want me to get her scarves and some few clothes, she said they be in the back bedroom there," and Etta walk splay-legged like a big bear toward the back of the house.

I already peeked in there. Just a single bed piled up with all kinds of clothes, and a couple of cardboard boxes with more rags and stuff. There was a busted bicycle on the floor with the handlebars off and only one tire.

Ma pick up the scarf that Helen Crier had yesterday. It been lying on the floor beside the rocking-chair.

"Look at this, Silas. Three sides of this here scarf been sewed up pretty but the fourth is all done funny with big stitches."

"I don't know nothing about sewing," I say.

Mad Etta come back with a couple of scrawny house-dresses over her arm, and carrying a square cardboard box.

"She got a whole box of scarves here, mostly made out of rags. Funny thing for a lady who never go nowhere to be making. Did she have a cat?" she say, looking at me hold on to the can of cat food.

"I don't know," say Ma. "I ain't been here for so long. Couple of months ago, the Crowchild girls, Denise and the little one, was around with a box full of yellow-coloured kittens. Wanted to give me one but I wouldn't take it. May-

114

be they came on out here."

Mad Etta sniff at the cat food and move the stuff around on the counter.

"If she had a kitten what do you suppose happened to it?" say Ma.

"Probably the dog got it," say Mad Etta moving back to the box of scarves.

"No," say Ma. "That's one thing I remember Helen telling me. Martin Crier wouldn't let her have a dog, or any pet, said they cost too much to feed."

"If they going to find anything upstairs I wish they'd hurry," say Mad Etta flapping her arms around herself.

"I wish I'd come to see her sometimes," say Ma. "It hard to imagine what lonesome is like with a big family, and neighbours."

Mad Etta light up a cigarette. "Help me pick out some scarves for her, Suzie. She say only to bring the bright-coloured ones."

I think about how I see Martin Crier come walk straight-backed out of the Bank of Montreal in Wetaskiwin, look solemn as a mountain in tan work clothes. I think maybe Mrs. Crier would of wanted a kitten.

Etta is pull out a couple of scarves that been folded up in the box, one is red silky stuff and the other purple, like from the back of a pair of boxer shorts. "Son of a bitch," say Etta and pull back from the box like she been bit or something. "See here what I found, Suzie," she say.

There is something wrapped up in a piece of yellow cloth.

"What's going on?" I ask.

"Get away, Silas," Ma say like she means it.

They whisper some. The yellow scarf got little dark spots on it, look to me like blood. "Squashed," I hear Etta say.

"Why would she do something like that?" say Ma.

"Wasn't her," say Etta. "I'd bet on it."

115

Ma and Mad Etta look at each other for what seem to me like an awful long time. Just then the men clump down the stairs and start for the door. Mad Etta be busy stuff the yellow scarf in the big old pocket of her coat.

"Was there a cat?" say the coroner, seeing the cat food where I left it at the front of the counter.

"The dog got it," say Mad Etta.

"I didn't see a dog anywhere," say Constable Marcel.

"Don't you know?" say Mad Etta, taking on the tone she use when she makes medicine. "Dogs know when somebody is die. They always run off after a death."

"Really?" say the coroner, curl up his lip at a dumb Indian lady.

"You guys mind if I take this here piece of bacon home?" say Mad Etta. "Don't look like nobody be cooking around here for a while."

"I don't see why not," say Corporal Greer.

"She's liable to be back sooner than you think," Constable Marcel say. "If she sticks to her story, it's going to be awfully hard to get a conviction without a motive. There's no sign of anybody else being around the place at all. Still, there's no solid evidence. I'm going to stay and look around the house again after we check the yard."

After they go out Mad Etta tosses the cat dish onto the pile of junk in the corner. Then she puts the tea bags back in the box on the counter. She shake out the beans into the slop pail.

We decide to go wait in the car. As we go out the door Ma picks up the frozen geranium. "Maybe like they say, Etta, this here plant got a lot stronger roots than we figure."

I REMEMBER HORSES

For Mickey

We had good intentions, all of us. Whole thing start when some salesman fellow from Calgary phone up Ben Stone-breaker's General Store here at Hobbema, say he got for Ben a bargain on frozen fish. When he hear the price Ben he smile so much his upper lip almost touch his nose but then he frown some when he hear that to get the good price he got to pick it up himself.

Ben wave me over from where me and my friend Frank Fence-post is leaning on the counter, drink Cokes and tease Ben's granddaughter about the number of freckles on her nose. There be three freezers down one wall of the store, white ones with black rubber lids feel like they made out of old car tires. These freezers is mostly empty except for when Ben stock up on ice cream and Sara Lee frozen cakes on the days when the UIC or welfare payments is due.

Ben orders up 300 pounds of that fish.

"Silas, I want you to drive to Calgary and pick up this here order for me," Ben say. He offer to pay gas for the truck and give me $20 for myself if I do. The truck belong to Blind Louis Coyote but Louis got a good heart and everyone who need the truck get to use it. As always when we decide to go someplace a lot of friends come along for the ride.

It been a whole year since we was to Calgary. Last time,

even though we don't mean to, we make a lot of trouble for my sister Illianna and her white man husband, Robert McGregor McVey. We got orders, in a letter in Illianna's own writing, that we is never to visit them again unless we is invited, and Illianna make it clear that the only ones that is ever going to get invited is me, Ma, and my brothers and sisters, but even then never more than two at a time.

My brother-in-law, Robert McGregor McVey, have a lot of bad feelings against Indians in general and in particular against us Indians from Hobbema, some of us who is his wife's relatives and some who isn't. I don't know what he expect when he marry an Indian girl, but it sure ain't that he married up with the whole family. We be the first ones to admit that the trouble ain't all Brother Bob's fault. The one time he come to the reserve he lose his car and Illianna get pregnant by her old boyfriend Eathen Firstrider, although Brother Bob never know that for sure. Times we visit them in the city, we lose their baby for a while and help Brother Bob get arrested, and another time we get them kicked out of their apartment and Brother Bob have some tattooing done on him that he hadn't planned on.

By the time we head out for Calgary there be whole lot of people in the truck including Blind Louis and his wife, my girlfriend Sadie One-wound, my friend Frank Fence-post and his girl Connie Bigcharles, Eathen Firstrider, Robert Coyote, Julie Scar and quite a few others. We have to leave our medicine lady Mad Etta at home, 'cause she weigh about 50 pounds more than the fish we picking up and there not be room for both on the trip back.

It is a sunny summer day and we can see the mountains from a long way off as we drive into Calgary. Even though the people in the back thump their hands on the roof of the cab every time we pass a town on the way down, and every time we pass a bar in the city, I drive right to the wholesale place 'cause I know it close at 5 o'clock and it important for us to get there on time. The Calgary Tower stand over the downtown like a can of Raid from a TV commercial, or if you was to put a scarf around its neck, like the Jolly Green Giant. It look out over the old part of downtown.

Soon as I stop the truck at the wholesale place the people in the back go running off to the Queen's Hotel which is only a couple of blocks away. We pick up the fish with no trouble. It come in three cardboard boxes be heavy to handle and cold to the touch.

"How long before this stuff thaw out?" I ask the wholesale man.

"If you wrap the boxes in that tarp you got there, why you have six or seven hours before you have to worry," he say.

It is less than a three-hour drive back to Hobbema so I figure we got a bit of time to spend. I sure hate having to worry about time. If it was just dry goods we was picking up why we could have us a little fun, take a day or two to get back.

While we having a beer at the Queen's somebody mention my brother-in-law and that start a whole lot of jokes about white men. The main thing wrong with Brother Bob is that he don't know how to make laughter, and Illianna, since she marry him, she don't anymore either. He sometimes call me Silas Verminskin, and call Eathen, Heathen Firstrider. Name jokes like that is funny when we say them to each other, but the trouble be that Brother Bob he don't speak his jokes with a happy heart.

I get to thinking of all the trouble we've had. "What if on the way home we was to take them a present?" I suggest.

"A peace offering," Frank say, and grin big. We decide it easiest to buy for a kid, so me and Frank and Sadie head off to the T. Eaton Department Store where we spend the $20

I am to earn for the trip on a soccer ball for little Bobby, Illianna and Bob's baby, who by now be over two years old. We don't know if he play soccer or not but we buy a ball with a red and white pattern that sure look pretty when it spin.

Take us another half-hour to round everybody up and get them back to the truck. Illianna and Brother Bob have their own home now. Illianna sent us a picture of it. It is way up at the North end of the city off the Crowchild Trail and their backdoor look up on one of the foothills what be a ripe wheat colour most of the year and have horses grazing around on it. Them foothills be the same shape and colour as girls' breasts and Frank he sometimes joke with Connie that he wish hers was that large.

The houses is all brand new, the streets not even paved yet, and many of the front yards be just piles of dirt. To be sure I don't offend Brother Bob or Illianna I park the truck across the street and about half a block past their place. Then I take the ball and go alone over to their house. They have a permanent sidewalk to their door and a paved driveway. Their lawn is smoothed and planted and furry grass is coming up, thin and soft as baby's hair.

I ring the bell about a dozen times but there ain't no answer. Looking around I can see people stare at me from out their windows while they pretend not to. Finally I go to the house next door. It is at least 50 feet away and just as big as Brother Bob's place. It is painted a dark green, the ugly colour of slough-scum. I smooth down my hair some and do up a couple of buttons on my jean jacket before I climb the steps but the eyes of the lady who answer the door still get big when she sees I'm an Indian.

"We come into town special to see the McVeys," I say and smile as nice as I know how at her.

"They're gone on holidays," she says. "Won't be back

for another week." She is young, small and blond and look like she just been washed in a hot tub for an hour or so. She be wearing a flowered housecoat and I can smell her soap clear through the screen door. While we talking she click over the lock on the door, I guess just in case I try to force myself into her house.

I'm just about to ask if she'll give the ball to Bobby when he get home, when I hear the truck roar and it come bump backward down the street, make a loud turn into Brother Bob's driveway, end with two wheels on the concrete and two wheels buried in the lawn. Frank grin out the truck window at me.

"They're not home, eh?" he yell. Two or three guys already got off the truck and is pushing at the rear while Frank rock it back and forth.

We can't get the truck to move. We tell Frank we going to put him under the back wheel to use for traction. But then everybody, and I count thirteen of us, get out of the truck. Then Robert Coyote and Eathen Firstrider practically lift the truck back on to the driveway. I still have the keys in my pocket and realize Frank must of wired the truck to start it. Frank he got this here natural talent for start up cars with no key and get in behind locked doors like they wasn't even there. He can open any door I ever seen with just his jackknife or maybe a paper clip. Too bad there ain't a way for him to use ability like that without always having RCMPs coming around to check him out.

"Gee, Silas, I wish somewhere there was a company would give me a credit card," he say after he seen on TV one time how a fellow open all kinds of doors by slipping one into locks.

By the time we got the truck unstuck, Frank he opened the front door and him and Connie is exploring like two cats in a strange cabin. I figure it won't do much harm if we just have a look at the inside of Illianna's new house.

Boy, it is one big place. It has about four levels and it smell like a hotel room in a fancy place like the Palliser Hotel or the Chateau Lacombe. Every bit of floor is covered with carpet, even the bathrooms. There is a bathroom on every level. I wonder if white people have to go more than Indians? Upstairs there is a real balcony with an iron railing and everything, where you can look down on the living-room. In the kitchen is one of them microwave ovens and just about every other electric appliance I ever seen anywhere.

"Where is this place?" say Blind Louis, stand in the middle of the living-room poke at a blue fuzzy chair with his white cane.

"This is the place where Illianna Ermineskin live with her white husband," his wife answer him.

"How come we didn't go up in the elevator like we did last time? And how come I can smell horses?" he wants to know.

"They moved to a new house," Mrs. Blind Louis answer, "and I don't know nothing about horses." But Louis is right, if you look out the back window there are a dozen or so horses graze high up on the hill. I guess Louis' nose must work better since his eyes quit seeing.

At first we creep around the house going, "Oooh," and "Ahhhh," and afraid to touch nothing. But we get used to it pretty quick. Connie and Frank turn on the TV, start the record player and crank up the sound. It is Eathen who finds the deepfreeze.

"What if we was to rest for a while and store the fish in here," he suggest.

It sound like a good idea and we cart the boxes of fish into the house and don't have to take too many packages out of the freezer to make room.

"I'm hungry," say Blind Louis. "What kind of host don't give his guests no food?"

"They ain't home," say Mrs. Blind Louis.

"There's steak in these packages," Sadie whisper to me.

If Illianna was home she'd offer at least some of us food, I figure. We toss a few steaks in the microwave oven and I pretend I know how to work it. It got a patch of numbers on the outside like the dial of a fancy phone. I make like I'm dialing a long distance number and pretty soon the steaks start to sizzle. About ten of us stand around and stare in the door of the oven.

"Not as good as the *Incredible Hulk*," say Frank, "but better than one of them documentaries," and we all have a good laugh. We give the first steaks to Mr. and Mrs. Blind Louis but when the smell get out we all discover we is hungry so we load in some more food to the oven and I try to remember what numbers I punched the first time that got the food to cook.

"No reason for us to go home tonight," say Robert Coyote. "Let's pretend we is city Indians," and he throw himself down backward on the big white chesterfield, like he was making a snow angel.

Some of us decide to go downtown and get a few cases of beer. When we stop in at the Queen's we meet some people used to live at Hobbema and we tell them about the party we going to make. They all look at us and wait with questions on their faces like a dog look when he waiting for you to throw a stick.

I know that inviting them ain't what Illianna and Brother Bob would want us to do, but it is what is good and right. If you got a place to be, then your friends should always be welcome. We load up the truck with another dozen or so people, including a guy called Trapper Benoît who be a Métis about seven foot tall, and head back up the Crowchild

Trail.

While we been gone a couple of bad things has happened. Connie and Frank gone in one of the fancy bathrooms and have themselves a hot shower in about a ton of bubble soap. They spill a little water on the floor, enough to soak their clothes and the carpet and I bet whatever is underneath, 'cause when I get there the soap suds is banked up against the walls like snowdrifts and if you look careful you can just make out the outline of the sink.

What is worse though is that since their clothes is wet they figure to dry them quick, but to do it they stuff them all in the microwave oven and punch a few numbers. Well, what we got when I get there is an oven full of melted running shoes, shirts, socks and jeans. Boy, when you open that oven door the smoke and smell that come out ain't gonna make anybody hungry.

"Smell like somebody branding cattle," say Blind Louis. Louis sit in a soft chair, got his feet up on a coffee table, have a beer and smoke his pipe. Louis is over 80 years old, work already on his third wife, who have a new baby just last year. Altogether he have close to twenty kids.

We make us a really good party. Everybody dance some, even Frank and Connie, who wear blankets around themselves just like real Indians. The music make the walls shake some but what is nice is that the house be far enough from its neighbours that no-one call the police which is what usually happen when Indians have a party in the city.

I mean, white people don't know nothing about making a party. Since I had my book printed up I been sent to some parties where there is mainly white people, and not ordinary white peoples but teachers, lawyers, university professors and other writers. They just sit around, drink and look sad, then they apologize all over you for drinking too much. They don't dance or yell up a good time, and except for a

124

writer once in a while, they hardly ever fist fight. I don't like white parties.

What I do wish is that this party been a little whiter. How was we to know that Trapper Benoît get mean when he drinks? Frank and Connie keep going up to that balcony over the living-room and then making loud war whoops they jump off and land on the white chesterfield. One time though, Frank he land right on Trapper Benoît. Trapper he brush Frank to the floor like he was a fly on his shoulder. Then he look mean at Eathen Firstrider. Him and Eathen give each other the evil eye for a while, then Trapper square off to Eathen.

"By God, I used to wrestle down at the Corral," he yell, "and I bust up five guys like you before breakfast every morning."

"I ain't afraid of no fucking buffalo like you," say Eathen as he is pulling his hunting knife out of his boot.

Well, Trapper Benoît I guess have a dislike of knives, but he still be mad. He make a quick move but instead of grab for Eathen he grab Frank who been minding his own business ever since he got knocked to the floor. Trapper pick Frank up by the blanket, spin him like he was swinging a cat and send him flying into the living-room curtains. There is the crunch of breaking glass and the drapes is sucked out by the wind. Frank fall back into the living-room, land right on the stereo set, do it a certain amount of damage.

It take six of us guys to pin down Trapper Benoît and the room get a little messed up while we doing it. We tie him up good with cord we cut off the drapes. Then we load him up in the truck and I drive all our friends downtown. They sure thank us a lot say how it is the best party they been to for a long time. We invite them back anytime. We haven't ever for sure said it ain't our own place they was visiting. The fresh air cooled Trapper off some. We untie him in the Imperial Hotel parking-lot and he shake our hands and thank us for the good party.

Next morning we cook breakfast on the stove because the microwave still full of melted clothes. We find a piece of plywood and block up the window some. We sure feel bad about the trouble we caused. To start with we all have good intentions.

"Wonder what we could do nice for Brother Bob?" I say.

Everybody is quiet until Blind Louis say, "Get him horses."

"Huh?" we all say.

"Best thing you can do for a man is to gift him with horses," say Louis. Some of us young guys look at each other and laugh until we see that he means it.

Horses don't mean much to anybody anymore. But they used to.

"I pay twelve horses for my first squaw," Blind Louis say. "Her father was called Buffalo Running Up A Hill. He was a Worthy Man. He have the hide of a white buffalo as the door-skin to his lodge. He dress his daughter in white buckskins; she was called Morning Light. . . ."

That remind me of something that happen I suppose ten years ago. My own papa he never even try to do much of nothing for his family. Louis Coyote though he be poor as us is always around home, try to make things as good as he can for his family, and I guess most important, he don't drink too much or get mean. One day me and Illianna and Joseph we out back of our cabin, ride on a poplar rail we set between two spruce stumps. We pretend it is a horse even though one end or other is always falling off the stumps. We got tied around the rail some binder-twine and we hold to it with one hand and wave in the air our other the way we seen cowboys do at the rodeo. Louis Coyote come by and look at us with his eyes the colour of skim milk. He listen

126

to us for a long time before he smile and say, "Horses is good.
I'm happy you play about horses. It is an Indian thing to
do." Then he smile and his eyes glow white like some rocks
do at night. "How'd you like if I make for you a wood horse,
solid built?" he say, and the three of us jump up and down
and yell, and Illianna, if I remember right, hug Blind Louis'
waist. He always wear a buckskin jacket with long thongs
hang down all around and there is always about him a soft
leather smell.

Louis Coyote always been one to keep a promise, even to
kids, and like he say he build us that horse. He don't have a
truck of his own then so he get one of them government
social workers who always wander around the reserve with
long faces say, "Is there anything I can do for you people?"
to drive him up to Wetaskiwin. He take Lazarus Battleford
along as his eyes and let a whole bunch of us kids ride in the
back. They have the social worker drive around to a place
where being built an addition to a school and they even get
the social worker to help load in the trunk of the car a saw-
horse, cement, nails and other stuff for building.

By the time we get back to the reserve that social worker
getting quite a bit suspicious. "Hey, it's okay," Lazarus
Battleford tell him. "Us Indians can't afford to go in the
butcher shop in Wetaskiwin to buy meat, so we hunt and
trap, right? Well, this is the same. We got no money to buy
building stuff so we go hunting for it and we don't even have
to use bullets to get it." Then Louis and Lazarus laugh into
each other's shoulders while the social worker keep his eyes
on the road.

Louis build that horse out behind our cabin. That make it
special. Louis got a dozen or so kids of his own but putting
the horse where he does make it mine and Illianna's and
Joseph's and be just like it was our own real one. We can say
who get to ride it and when.

First, Blind Louis dig holes in the ground and pour in around the legs of the saw-horse, cement. Then when the cement hooves hold the saw-horse tight, like a scared kid hugging its mother's neck, he start with the head.

I can still see him walk off toward the muskeg. It be a couple of hundred yards downhill and been burned over a lot of years ago. He choose from the muskeg a piece of wood, weathered grey except for some charred spots, and using his jackknife to cut and his fingers to feel, he make the head of a horse. It take him quite a few days. His hands and face would get black from the burnt wood and sometimes the soot would get on his hair that even then was the colour of dandelion fluff.

In the meantime us kids was already riding the horse that we named Pansy on account of some of those little flowers with faces like old men grew wild on the ground by our feet. Louis nailed what was left of a saddle to the middle of the saw-horse and he run some real reins, from his own harness, to the front so we got something to hold on to. Them reins is real leather and long enough to wind around our hands the way real cowboys do.

I am there alone the day that Louis come over to nail the head to the body. That piece of burned deadfall look really like a horse. The nostrils flare and it got eyes wild as the meanest mustang. But it is just a head. It is hard to explain when I watch him feel around with his big scarred hands find the right spot to nail it down, I guess it is that I feel that me, a little kid, know more than a man like Louis, because when he got it all in place I say, "Look, it got no neck," and I grab his hand and force it to feel high up along her wooden spine.

Then Louis look across at me, his white eyes like moonlight. "I remember horses," he say. "I wasn't always blind."

And I realize, the way a kid do, that I make a fool of myself, but I don't say nothing. And neither do Louis. The best thing I figure is to show I like the horse so I jump in the saddle, yell like three rodeo cowboys, lots louder than I have to, as I pretend I having a hard ride. Louis head off toward his cabin and it seem to me that his shoulders is slumped over just a bit.

All us Ermineskin kids and all Louis' kids and the Fenceposts, One-wounds, Firstriders, Wolfchilds and a few other families ride that horse Pansy all summer and fall until one day when my papa be drunk and meaner than usual he chop it up with the axe and stuff it in the oil-drum stove to heat the cabin.

". . . I steal them twelve horses all by myself and in early morning drive them to the lodge of Buffalo Running Up A Hill. Then I take Morning Light to my own lodge." Louis' voice sort of trail off and none of us is laughing anymore.

Horses used to be most important thing there was to Indians. They mean freedom, and power, and strength, but mostly freedom. I remember Louis, not long ago, tapping his truck with his white cane and saying, "You ever know that truck to bring you home safe when you was lost or too tired to drive it?"

Guess we all heard Louis say things like that. Even though we know horses don't mean much now we decide to make them important today. We find some extension cord in the garage that we cut up and Eathen, Robert, me, Frank and the other guys climb up that hill behind the house and catch us a couple of horses. They is pretty tame and we lead them down into Brother Bob's yard. We tie them to the back screen door. "Good horses," Louis says, running his old brown hands along their necks. And he smile at us.

"You know," Frank whisper to me, "I bet Brother Bob would rather have a boat."

I know this is true 'cause I've heard him and Illianna talk about it. "Hey, we get him one of those too," I say.

We head off downtown and look around until we find us a big boat dealer. They got a whole block of parking-lot covered in nothing but boats, and they got the concrete under them painted a bright blue so people can pretend they is in the water. We don't know much about boats but we pick out one that already sitting on a trailer and looks expensive. It have a windshield, lots of red and white plastic all over it, and a motor hang over the back that is, so a sign say, 150 horse power.

We learn a long time ago that to get along with white men you got to act like you know what you doing. They don't expect Indians to do that and they is always surprised when it happen. The word for it was taught me by my English Instructor down at the Tech School in Wetaskiwin. It is panache. We just back the truck up to the boat and since we got no trailer hitch we tie a rope to each side of the boat trailer and a couple of guys stand in each corner of the truck box and hold on tight.

"Where are you guys going with that boat?" a salesman in a blue jacket and sailor's cap say to us.

"Don't you know?" we say back. "Big Indian pow-wow down to St. George's Island. Premier Lougheed gonna get his picture took from this here boat along with a whole bunch of Indian chiefs. Get your company's name in the newspapers and everything," and we just keep easing the boat off the lot while the salesman stand there scratching his head, scared to stop us but afraid not to.

We sure get a lot of funny looks as we head up Crowchild Trail again with that boat swinging from side to side like a big red and white fish.

I don't have much luck trying to back that boat into Brother Bob's driveway. It go every way but where I want it to. We end up with the boat kind of sideways on the lawn and the truck stuck axle deep in the new grass.

While Robert and Eathen trying to dig out the truck I find that the horses has pulled the screen door off the back of the house and be grazing their way back up the hill dragging the door behind them.

"Bring them inside," say Louis, when we lead them back. "Smart man use the lower part of this place for a barn."

So we lead them horses down the two or three steps into the basement. I fill up the bath tub in case they want a drink, and Sadie and Connie carry in armfulls of grass and put beside the furnace.

Blind Louis whack his cane on the outside of the house. "Illianna's husband will be happy. You can't give a man no better gift than horses."

I suspect it is more Louis who is happy than anyone else. I leave the back door open so them horses can go home any time they want to. The red and white soccer ball is spin slow in that bathtub full of water that slop every so often on the floor.

Just to make sure the fish stay fresh we load the freezer up in the truck. I think about leaving Illianna a little note say we bring it back next time we come to Calgary and that we hope they like the boat and the horses and the soccer ball. But I don't.

As we finally leaving I see that white lady peeking out of her door.

"Probably you shouldn't tell them we was here," I say.

"They'll guess," the white lady say through the screen door.

SUITS

George Longvisitor is the kind of man who go through life like he was being dragged behind a bull. He is big and tall and strong. You know what he is like if you ever walked by one of those electric transformer stations at night. They make a strong hum and cause the ground to shake gentle. George Longvisitor do the same to people around him.

My girl Sadie One-wound and me is at Longvisitor's house when George come home. He been away for a month on a welding job way up in British Columbia. His one-ton truck with the welding unit on the back come bumping up the road, snow boiling out behind it like dust. George bound out of the truck as if someone chasing him and up the steps to the front door three at a time.

George likes being an Indian but he wants to make a good living too. His house was built by Indian Affairs and he fixed it up by adding on an extra room and a garage. He is not like a lot of people who get those houses. Many see how fast they can wreck them: like Moses Longpre who chopped a hole in the wall of his new house so he could water his horses in the bathtub.

George have to duck his head when he come through the door and he bring in with him a rush of cold air. The four kids and Mrs. Longvisitor all run to hug him. He is wearing a green mackinaw, khaki pants and a red-plaid hunting hat with the earflaps down. He has brought presents for everybody: for the four boys, hunting hats just like his only each in different colours, and for Mrs. Longvisitor an electric mixer must of cost close to a hundred dollars and got bright buttons sticking out of paint white as new snow. Under his arm he got a long, lean box of the kind that come from clothing stores.

"Hey, Silas," he say to me, and almost crush my hand in both of his. "If I'd knowed you was here I'd of brought you something."

"No need for that," I say, but I know he means what he say.

"Hell, when you got the money you use it, right? Money's only good for what you can buy with it," and George slap my back and give Sadie a hug enough to squash her.

George like to tell the story about when he was young and used to walk around Wetaskiwin and look at the big houses. "I seen that all the white men that owned them worked full-time at something, and I figured I was just as strong as any white man and could work just as hard. So I went down to the Corrigal Welding Shop and just hung around until one day somebody said, 'Hey, Kid, hand me that,' or 'Help me lift this,' and before long I had a job and I learn everything there was to know about welding. After I got my ticket I priced a welding unit and put half my wages in the bank until I had enough to buy it. Hell, most guys spend half their cheque on booze anyway, so all I missed out on was a few headaches," and he laugh and hug up his boys who be about from four to ten years old, and his wife Ramona too, all in a big armful, and they laugh and make happy sounds.

Him and Ramona and all the kids belong to the Pente-costal Church in Wetaskiwin: it is one of them places where church is happy instead of fearful, where everybody holler

"Praise the Lord," and sing up a storm and shake hands on each other. I been there a time or two and all the friendliness kind of make me nervous, but at least that church think its people are smart enough to understand and share in the services. I always think of bright yellows and greens and oranges when I think of them, not like the browns, greys and blacks of the Catholics.

"Hell, I don't believe much of what they preach about," say George, "but they don't believe in drinking, and if going there keep even one of my boys away from liquor, then it going to be worth it."

George insists that Sadie and me stay for supper, which is stew and biscuits and which George have about seven helpings of.

"Let's go up and see Pop," he say after dinner. Pop is Eli Longvisitor, George's father. Eli is really old, like 90 or more. He used to live in with George and the family but George was always taking him on trips with him when he went off on welding jobs, and hauling him to church and for walks. Eli said it was too hard on him and too noisy with all the kids, TV and stereo. "You kids come too," George say to us. "Pop don't get many visitors. He'll be glad to see you."

But first George hustle off to the bedroom with that box what the kids have been curious over ever since he got home. In a few minutes he come out and he is all dolled up in a white shirt, blue tie and a shiny blue suit that is even nicer than the one Chief Tom Crow-eye wear. We all get treated to the smell of new cloth.

"Three hundred and twenty-five dollars," say George, holding an arm out in front of him so he can admire the material, smile like he looking at a new baby. "When you got the money . . ." he say again and nod his head.

The Sundance Retirement Home in Wetaskiwin is where old Eli is at. Can't imagine anyone liking to live in that place.

134

The rooms is tiny and green painted, the floors are dark brown linoleum and the whole place smell of Lysol and hotel soap. The halls are full of old people in wheelchairs who keep their arms and legs in funny positions like dolls what been throwed in a corner. Some yell a lot, toss their bodies around and have seat belts to keep them in their chairs. Eli ain't that far gone. He still walk to the dining-room for his meals even though he had a few strokes that twist one side of his face real strange like a big hand grabbed at one cheek and pulled down. And before he speak it seem like he take a very long time to decide what he want to say.

"Papa," George boom out, after we knocked at Eli's door and the old man eventually answer it. George grab up Eli's hand what is gnarled and covered in spots until it look like spruce bark, remembering at the last second not to squeeze it so hard as to bust anything. Eli have a puzzled look on his face. He is short with bandy legs and walk with two canes and stiff bones, so he turn a little from side to side with each step. He have sunk cheeks where his teeth used to be and the flesh has melted off his neck until the skin hang loose like innertube. His nose be soft and flat as if it had no bone in it at all. One brown eye got film over it like smoke from a brush fire. His shoulders been broad at one time and his chest under his plaid shirt is still deep.

George is about two feet taller than Eli but it is still easy to see they related. Eli must see in George what he was like young, and I guess it is for George like looking into the future when he stare at his father.

"How do you like my suit, Papa?" George say, shoving his sleeve under the old man's nose. Eli is still trying to close the door and get used to his grandkids tugging at him, and looking with his one good eye at Sadie and me to see if he should know us. Finally he reach out his old hand and stroke the suit, careful, like he would an ermine pelt. Real slowly he take a bit of the cloth between his thumb and finger.

"Feel as though it been greased," he say real slow in Cree, and he smile as much as he can. "Look like it been touched by the Northern Lights."

Eli was at one time chief of our tribe. There be a picture down at Blue Quills Hall of him and Prime Minister Mackenzie King and King George at a big pow-wow.

I remember George telling the story of when he brought home a shiny white refrigerator from Simpsons-Sears store in Wetaskiwin. He claim he was the first Indian on the reserve to own one. When it was all hooked up he showed it to Eli. "He walked around it looking at it from all angles like it was something that come from the moon. When he put his hand inside the freezer compartment he looked at me and said, 'You have captured winter and locked it in this box.'"

"Do you like it?" George keep asking Eli about the suit.

"It is very fine," Eli say. "You could trade it in for many ponies."

George look a little hurt. I think he would like for Eli to be more excited.

"I got something for you in the truck, Papa," say George, and he move for the door, ducking his head as he leave.

All the way up in the truck, the four of us sitting in the cab, the kids riding in the back, George been talking about Eli. "I got to do something to put some life back in him. He's gonna mildew if he stays like he is. You ought to of seen him stack cordwood."

"Why don't you just let him be old?" Ramona say. "Some people are happy to get old."

"Not me," booms George. "Hell, that old man used to ride with war parties. He's who I learned from. He rode range until he was 80 and trapped and hunted . . ."

George come striding back into the room. "I was gonna buy you a suit just like mine," he say to Eli. "Then as I was

136

looking out the window of the men's store in Prince George, I seen a store across the street that sell Indian clothes." George is carrying a package that is half as tall as he is and wrapped in thick brown paper. It got a lot of scuff marks on it where it bounced in the truck and where the kids been picking at it on the way up. "I said to myself, what kind of clothes would my papa like? And then I go over there and have me a look around."

George toss the package on the bed where it bounce up like a five-year-old. Eli look at it but don't make no effort to open it so George do the work. He tear off the thick outside wrapper and show up a clothing box like his suit come in only bigger.

George take out first a headdress of bright blues, greens, yellows and reds. It is not just come to the shoulders but run all the way down the back of whoever wear it. There is a story that Chief Tom Crow-eye went to a tailor shop in Edmonton and had the tribal bonnet shortened because he is so short that it drag on the ground behind him. Eli make kind of a feeble smile and touch the feathers with his mottled old hands.

Out of the box George take a wooden breastplate, a shield decorated with feathers, leggings and moccasins heavy with coloured beads. The moccasins fill the room with a smoky leather smell. There also be two rattles covered in cowhide.

"Kind of stuff a real chief should wear," say George.

Eli Longvisitor still have that puzzled frown on his face. He pick up a moccasin, hold it to his nose, and his toothless mouth make a smile and there be some light in his one good eye. "Ah," he say, then pause for a long time. "When I was young . . ." I thought for sure he was going to say something but his voice trail off and the light fade out of his eye like the tail-lights of a car pulling away from you fast.

He look real confused at George. "What do you want me

to do with all this?" He spread his twisted old hands out in front of him.

"I want you to live," George say loud enough that it bring a nurse into the room, and he face his papa, his own hands big as baseball gloves, spread out in front of him.

Nobody except George was very surprised when a couple of days later Eli Longvisitor died.

There is a prayer service at Oberholtzer's Funeral Home in Wetaskiwin. George decide to give the old man a Christian burial, I guess cause it make *him* feel good. We stand around kind of uneasy, separated from the coffin by a scarlet rope, our fingerprints like frosty breath on the chrome tops of the posts that keep us from Eli Longvisitor.

George tap me on the shoulder and make a motion with his finger for me to follow him. He duck his head as we leave the funeral home and it kind of hard to get used to the bright sun of outside and the sounds our boots make on the frozen sidewalks after all the carpets inside.

I don't say nothing 'cause I figure George will talk if he wants to. We get in his truck and drive down to the graveyard. The caretaker, old Felicien Cyr, is hacking away with a pick, and the air is thick with the smell of burned straw what be used to thaw the ground.

"You never gonna get that done in time for the funeral," George say.

"Shouldn't of died in the wintertime," is the way Felicien make an answer. He is wearing a mackinaw, heavy leather mitts and move so slow he look like a television replay.

George stomp around in a circle for a couple of minutes kicking lumps of earth. Then he take up a shovel and jump down into the grave. His body move like it was a powered machine and he don't even notice that he is wearing his new $325 suit he is so busy slinging clods of dirt over his shoulder at the glaring blue of the sky.

PRETEND DINNERS

For Barbara Kostynyk

It was Oscar Stick she married. The thing that surprise me most about Oscar and Bonnie getting together is that Oscar be a man who don't really like women, and Bonnie seem to me a woman who need more love than anybody I ever knowed.

She was Bonnie Brightfeathers to start with and a girl who always been into this here Women's Lib stuff. She been three years older than me for as long as I can remember. That age make quite a difference at times. When she was eighteen she don't even talk to a kid like me, but now that she's 23 and I'm 20, it don't seem to make any difference at all.

Bonnie Brightfeathers graduate the grade twelve class at the Residential School with really good report cards. She hold her head up, walk with long steps like she going someplace, and she don't chase around with guys or drink a lot. Her and Bedelia Coyote is friends and they always say they don't need men for nothing.

"A woman without a man be like a fish without a bicycle," Bedelia say all the time. She read that in one of these *MS* magazines that she subscribe to, and she like to say it to my

139

girlfriend Sadie One-wound when she see us walk along the road have our arms around each other.

After high school Bonnie get a job with one of these night patrol and security companies in Wetaskiwin. Northwest Security and Investigations is the right name. She wear a light brown uniform and carry on her hip in a holster what everybody say is a real gun. She move away from her parents who got more kids than anything else except maybe beer bottles what been throwed through the broke front window of their cabin and lay in the yard like cow chips. She move from the reserve to Wetaskiwin after her first pay cheque. Pretty soon she got her own little yellow car and an apartment in a new building at the end of 51st Avenue.

All this before she was even nineteen. It was almost a year later that I got to know her good. A government-looking letter come to the reserve for her and her father ask me to take it up to Wetaskiwin the next time I go. That same night I went in Blind Louis Coyote's pickup truck and Bonnie invite me up to her apartment after I buzzed the talk-back machine in the lobby.

It be an apartment where the living-room/bedroom be all one. The kitchen is about as big as most closets but she got the whole place fixed up cheerful: soft cushions all over the place, lamps with coloured bulbs and pretty dishes. She got too a record player and a glass coffee table with chrome legs. The kitchen table be so new that it still smell like the inside of a new car. There are plants too, hang on a wool rope from the ceiling and brush my shoulder when I cross the room to sit on her sofa. Whole apartment ain't big enough to swing a cat in, but it is a soft, warm place to be, like the inside of a sleeping bag.

Bonnie is a real pretty person remind me some of my sister Illianna. She got long hair tied in kind of a ponytail on each side of her head and dark eyes just a little too big for her face.

Her skin is a browny-yellow colour like furniture I seen in an antique-store window. She is a lot taller than most Indian girls and real slim. She wear cut-off jeans and a lime-green blouse the night I come to see her.

She give me a beer in a tall glass. I don't even get to see the bottle except when she take it out of the fridge. She put out for us some peanuts in a sky-blue coloured dish the shape of a heart while she talk to me about how happy she is.

This is about the time that I write down my first stories for Mr. Nichols. Being able to do something that I want to do sit way off in the future like a bird so high in the sky that it be just a speck, but I can understand how proud Bonnie feel to see her life turning out good.

"Someday, Silas, I'm going to have me a whole big house. I babysit one time for some people in Wetaskiwin who got a living-room bigger than this whole apartment." She pour herself a beer and come sit down beside me.

"You know what they teached us at the Home Economics class in high school? About something called gracious living. Old Miss Lupus, she show us how to set a table for a dinner party of eight. She show us what forks to put where and learned us what kind of wine to serve with what dish."

Bonnie got at the end of her room the top half of a cupboard with doors that are like mirrored sunglasses, all moonlight coloured and you can sort of see yourself in them. When she tell me the cupboard is called a hutch I make jokes about how many rabbits she could keep in there.

"I remember Bedelia Coyote saying, 'Hell, we have a dinner party for fifteen every night, but we only got eleven plates so the late ones get to wait for a second sitting, if the food don't run out first."

After a while Bonnie show me the inside of that cupboard. She got two dinner plates be real white and heavy, two sets of silver knives, spoons and fat and thin forks, two wine glasses with stems must be six inches long, and four or five bottles of wine and liquor. The bottles be all different colours and shapes.

"Most everybody make fun of that stuff Miss Lupus teach us, but I remember it all good and I'm gonna use it some day. One time Sharon Fence-post asked, 'What kind of wine do you serve with Kraft Dinner?' and Miss Lupus try to give her a straight answer, but everybody laugh so hard we can't hear what she say."

Bonnie take down the bottles from the cabinet to show me. "I buy them because they look pretty. See, I never even crack the seals," and she take out a tall bottle of what could be lemon pop except the label say, *Galliano*. She got too a bottle of dark green with a neck over a foot long and it have a funny name that I have to write down on the back of a matchbook, *Valpolicella*.

"We put on pretend dinners up there at the school. They got real fancy wine glasses, look like a frosted window, and real wine bottles except they got in them only water and food colouring. We joke about how Miss Lupus and Mr. Gortner, the principal, drink up all the real wine before they fill up the bottles for us to pretend with. Vicki Crowchild took a slug out of one of them bottles, then spit it clean across the room and say, 'This wine tastes like shit.' Miss Lupus suspended her for two weeks for that.

"See this one," Bonnie say, and show me a bottle that be both a bottle and a basket, all made of glass and filled with white wine. "Rich people do that," she say, "put out wine bottles in little wood baskets. They sit it up on the table just like a baby lay in a crib."

There is a stone crock of blue and white got funny birds fly around on it, and one that be stocky and square like a bottle of Brut Shaving Lotion, and be full of a bright green drink called *Sciarda*. I'd sure like to taste that one sometime.

It is like we been friends, Bonnie and me, for a long time, or better than friends, maybe a brother and sister. Bonnie got in her lamp soft coloured light bulbs that make the room kind of golden. She put Merle Haggard on the record player and we talk for a long time. Later on, my friends Frank and Rufus give me a bad time 'cause I stay there maybe three hours and leave them wait in the truck. They tease me about what we maybe done up there, but I know we are just friends and what anybody else think don't matter.

"Sit up to the table here, Silas, and I make for you a pretend dinner," Bonnie say. She put that heavy plate, white as new snow, in front of me, and she arrange the knife and other tools in the special way she been taught.

"Put your beer way off to the side there. Beer got no place at pretend dinners," and she set out the tall wine glasses and take the glass bottle and basket and make believe she fill up our glasses. "Know what we having for dinner?"

"Roast moose," I say.

Bonnie laugh pretty at that, but tell me we having chicken or maybe fish 'cause when you having white wine you got to serve only certain things like that with it.

"I remember that, the next time we have a bottle in the bushes outside Blue Quills Hall on Saturday night," I tell her.

Bonnie make me a whole pretend dinner, right from the things she say is appetizers to the roast chicken stuffed with rice. "What do you want for dessert?" she ask me. When I say chocolate pudding, she say I should have a fancy one like strawberry shortcake or peaches with brandy. "Might as well have the best when you making believe."

I stick with chocolate pudding. I like the kind that come in a can what is painted white inside.

"Some of this here stuff is meant to be drunk after dinner," Bonnie say, waving the tall yellow bottle that got the picture of an old-fashioned soldier on the label. "I ain't got the right glasses for this yet. Supposed to use tiny ones no bigger than the cap off a whisky bottle. This time you got to pretend both the liquor and glass. Miss Lupus tell us that people take their after-dinner drinks to the living-room, have their cigarette there and relax their stomach after a big meal."

I light up Bonnie's cigarette for her and we pretend to relax our stomachs.

"I'm gonna really do all this one day, Silas. I'm gonna get me a man who likes to share real things with me, but one who can make believe too."

"Thought you and Bedelia don't like men?"

"Bedelia's different from me. She really believe what she say, and she's strong enough to follow it through. I believe women should have a choice of what they do, but that other stuff, about hating men, and liking to live all alone, for me at least that just be a front that is all pretend like these here dinners."

She say something awful nice to me then. We talking in Cree and it be a hard language to say beautiful things in. What Bonnie say to me come up because we carried on talking about love. I say I figure most everybody find someone to love at least once or twice.

"How many people you know who is happy in their marriage?" Bonnie say.

"Maybe only one or two," I tell her.

"I don't want no marriage like I seen around here. For me it got to be more. I want somebody to twine my nights and days around, the way roses grow up a wire fence."

When I tell her how pretty I figure that is her face break open in a great smile and the dimples on each side of her mouth wink at me. I wish her luck and tell her how much I enjoy that pretend dinner of hers. Bonnie got a good heart.

I hope she find the kind of man she looking for.

That's why it be such a surprise when she marry Oscar Stick.

Oscar is about 25. He is short and stocky with bowed legs. He walk rough, drink hard and fist-fight anybody who happen to meet his eye. He like to stand on the step of the Hobbema General Store with his thumbs in his belt loops. Oscar can roll a cigarette with only one hand and he always wear a black felt hat that make him look most a foot taller than he really is. He rodeo all summer and do not much in the winter.

Oscar be one of those mean, rough dudes who like to see how many women he can get and then he brag to everybody and tell all about what he done with each one.

"A woman is just a fuck. The quicker you let her know that the better off everybody is." Oscar say that to us guys one night at the pool hall. He is giving me and my friend Frank Fence-post a bad time 'cause we try to be mostly nice to our girlfriends.

"Always let a woman know all you want to do is screw her and get to hell away from her. It turns them on to think you're like that. And everyone thinks they is the one gonna change your mind. You should see how hard they try, and the only way a woman know to change you is to fuck you better . . ." and he laugh, wink at us guys, and light up a cigarette by crack a blue-headed match with his thumbnail.

Guess Bonnie must of thought she could change him.

"Bedelia's never once said 'I told you so' to me. She been a good friend." It is last week already and it is Bonnie Stick talking to me.

Not long after that time three years ago when her and Oscar married, her folks got one of them new houses that the Indian Affairs Department build up on the ridge. After things start going bad for Oscar and Bonnie they move into

Brightfeathers' old cabin on the reserve.

"It was Bedelia who got the welfare for me when Oscar went off to rodeo last summer and never sent home no money."

I met Bonnie just about dusk walking back to her cabin from Hobbema. She carrying a package of teabags, couple of Kraft Dinner and a red package of DuMaurier cigarettes. She invite me to her place for tea.

We've seen each other to say hello to once in a while but we never have another good visit like we did in Wetaskiwin. I am just a little bit shy to talk to her 'cause I know about her dreams and I only have to look at her to tell that things turned out pretty bad so far.

She still wear the tan-coloured pants from her uniform but by now they is faded, got spots all over them, and one back pocket been ripped off. Bonnie got a tooth gone on her right side top and it make her smile kind of crooked. She got three babies and look like maybe she all set for a fourth by the way her belly bulge. I remember Oscar standing on the steps of the store saying, "A woman's like a rifle: should be kept loaded up and in a corner."

She boil up the tea in a tin pan on the stove. We load it up with canned milk and sugar. Bonnie look over at the babies spread out like dolls been tossed on the bed. The biggest one lay on her stomach with her bum way up in the air. "We got caught the first time we ever done it, Oscar and me," and she make a little laugh as she light up a cigarette. "This here coal-oil lamp ain't as fancy as what I had in the apartment, eh?"

We talk for a while about that apartment.

"I really thought it would be all right with Oscar. I could of stayed working if it weren't for the babies. They took back the car and all my furniture 'cause I couldn't pay for it. At first Oscar loved me so good, again and again, so's I didn't mind living in here like this," and she wave her hand around the dark cabin with the black woodstove and a few pieces of broke furniture. "Then he stopped. He go off to the rodeo for all summer, and when he is around he only hold me when he's drunk and then only long enough to make himself happy.

"I shouldn't be talking to you like this, Silas. Seems like every time I see you I tell you my secrets."

I remind her about those pretty words she said to me about twining around someone. She make a sad laugh. "You can only pretend about things like that . . . they don't really happen," and she make that sad laugh again. "Sometimes I turn away from him first just to show I don't give a care for him either. And sometimes I feel like I'm as empty inside as a meadow all blue with moonlight, and that I'm gonna die if I don't get held. . . ."

Bonnie come up to me and put her arms around me then. She fit herself up close and put her head on my chest. She hang on to me so tight, like she was going to fall a long way if she was to let go. I feel my body get interested in her and I guess she can too 'cause we be so close together. I wonder if she is going to raise her face up to me and maybe fit her mouth inside mine the way girls like to do.

But she don't raise her face up. "It ain't like you think," she say into my chest. "I know you got a woman and I got my old man, wherever he is. It's just that sometimes . . ." and her voice trail off.

I kind of rub my lips against the top of her head. Her arms been holding me so long that they started to tremble. "I charge up my batteries with you, Silas. Then I can go along for another while and pretend that everything is going to be okay. Hey, remember the time that I made up the pretend dinner for you? I still got the stuff," she say, and take her arms from around me. From under the bed she bring out a cardboard box say Hoover Vacuum Cleaner on the side, and take out that tall wine bottle, and the heavy white plates, only one been broke and glued back together so it got a scar clean across it.

She clear off a space on the table and set out the plates and wine glasses. One glass got a part broken out of it, a V shape, like the beak of a bird. The wine bottles is dusty and been empty for a long time.

"Oscar drink them up when he first moved in with me, go to sleep with his head on the fancy table of mine," Bonnie say as she tip up the tall bottle. She laugh a little and the dimples show on each side of her mouth.

"I'll take the broke glass," she say, "though I guess it not make much difference if we don't have no wine. If you're hungry, Silas, I make some more tea and there's biscuits and syrup on the counter."

"No thanks," I say. "We don't want to spoil these here pretend dinners by having food."

WEASELS AND ERMINES

"Silas, I know you're telling me the truth," Mr. Nichols say to me, "but," and his face get all red like it do when he have to say something that embarrass him, "I wouldn't tell a story like that to anyone, whether it's true or not. Not if you ever want to get out of here."

Mr. Nichols, my counsellor and English teacher from the Tech School in Wetaskiwin, wear a blue suit that don't fit him very good; he got stooped shoulders, gold-rimmed glasses, and a gold tooth in the front of his face that make sparks when he smile. He is about the kindest white man I know, so I always try to believe what he tell me.

I'm in jail and the RCMP are thinking about charging me and Mad Etta with doing a murder on RCMP Constable Chretien, Wade Gaskell and his friend Clete Iverson.

I remember one time Mr. Nichols saying to our class at the Tech School, "Telling the truth means never having to run away from anything," but I'm not so sure. If I tell the truth of what really happened I'm pretty certain they put me in the crazy place down to Ponoka where I'd never be able to run from anything again, and I know that ain't what Mr. Nichols had in mind. But it seem to me that every time an Indian tell the truth it get him in more trouble than if he lied.

The first bad thing was when Wade Gaskell start hanging around Florence Rockthunder. Wade Gaskell is about as bad a dude as it possible to be. He is white, come from Wetaskiwin where his daddy own a big business sell and service tractors. He's got a kind of gold-coloured hair come about to his shoulders, pale blue eyes set wide apart, a nose that been broke a couple of times, and a mouth of bright red, pretty as a girl's.

Wade wear tight jeans and a denim vest show off muscles what been tattooed in quite a few places. When he ain't in the bar of the Alice Hotel or at the Passtime Pool Hall in Wetaskiwin, he drive around in a customized car make as much noise as three Mack trucks stuck in gumbo.

Indian girls usually know enough to stay away from Wade. And if any Indian girl should stay clear of him it is Florence Rockthunder 'cause she got a secret he would sure want to know if he could.

A couple of years ago Wade's brother, Clarence Gaskell, did a murder on an Indian girl name of Little Margaret Wolfchild, and when he got only 90 days in Fort Saskatchewan jail for doing it, some of us Indians even up the score by making him dead. RCMPs never find out who rubbed out Clarence. There was only five girls who know all about it and me who guessed. One girl is dead, one moved away to Ontario, one is my girlfriend, Sadie One-wound, another is Robert Coyote's woman, Bertha Bigcharles, and the last was Florence Rockthunder.

First time I seen them together was at the Alice Hotel in Wetaskiwin. It was a Friday night and a bunch of us was having a few beers. About 11 o'clock in come Florence, Wade and a white couple, friends of Wade's I guess. They sit down across the bar from us and order up a table full of beer. They must of come from the Canadian Legion because it is easy to see they is all a little drunk except Florence who is a lot. She sit with her legs out in the aisle and her face that is wide and flat be kind of out of focus, like a buttered slice of brown bread. Florence wearing jeans, and a denim jacket over a red sweater. She is tall for a girl and got big hands and feet.

They laugh a lot at that table. Florence light up a cigarette, take a big drink of beer, spill some down the front of her. Wade point at what she do and they laugh some more.

When Wade finally go to the bathroom a bunch of us go over quick to that table try to get Florence away from there. There is me and Sadie, Frank and Connie, Robert Coyote and Bertha Bigcharles, at least. We kind of form a half-circle around Florence, have our backs to the white couple at the table.

"You know who that is you're with?" we say.

Florence smile kind of silly.

"That's Wade Gaskell," we say, though we pretty sure she know already.

"Come on," say Connie, and pull at Florence's sleeve.

"I can sit with anybody I want to," say Florence and give us a mean look.

We is just about to haul her away with us when Wade Gaskell come back.

"What have we got here," he say, "a war party?" and he give us a mean laugh.

There is enough of us to fight him and win but we don't want that if we can help it. Everybody know that Wade carry a knife and that he got at least a shotgun and a rifle in his truck, and that he is the kind of guy to use them.

"We want Florence to come to a party with us," say Robert.

"Flo here is my lady tonight," Wade say. He put his arm around Florence's shoulders and squeeze and she smile stupid at him like she can't see no-one else. "Ain't that

151

right?" he say to Florence who smile some more, then turn her chair so her back be to us.

We go away then but it sure spoil the evening for us. I remember something else Mr. Nichols say one time about a chain being only so strong as its weakest link, and that worry me.

They give to me a Legal Aid lawyer with a name I can't remember. He is only about five foot tall, look like he might be made out of bread dough. He have a little bit of curly blond hair on the back half of his head, and teacup ears that be bright pink as a rabbit's. His glasses is so thick that all I see is a blue blur for eyes and the silver rims glint in the light like new polished chrome on a car.

Just for fun I tell him the story like it really happen. He don't say nothing but the blue behind his glasses just get bigger and brighter as I talk. Then he shake hands on me and trot away real fast. It been three days and I ain't seen him again.

Wade Gaskell and his friend Clete Iverson got an apartment in Wetaskiwin and it appear that Florence Rockthunder is moved right in there 'cause she don't even come home to the reserve for a change of clothes in over a week.

Sadie and Bertha say they seen her shopping in Saan Department Store in Wetaskiwin one afternoon; she been drinking already and was buying up some lipsticks and jewellery with a twenty dollar bill she say Wade gave her to spend just on herself.

"Are you crazy?" Bertha say to her. "That guy's gonna make you say things you don't want to."

"Leave me alone," Florence say back to them. "Wade don't care no more about what happened to his brother. He told me so. You just leave me alone," and she take a sample perfume bottle from the counter and spray herself good. "Wade likes me and I'm gonna live in with him for as long

152

as he wants," and she turn her back and walk away.

It is only a day or two later that Constable Chretien from the RCMP come nose around the reserve ask questions about who rubbed out Clarence Gaskell. And this time he talk to Bertha Bigcharles and he ask her about Sadie but by that time we had her hid away at Firstrider's cabin. You can bet Constable Chretien didn't get the idea to start asking questions again all by himself. Even for an RCMP, Constable Chretien is pretty dumb. He is from Quebec and he speak English about as bad as we do, and he always have a kind of surprised look on his face like he just been kicked in the ass by a big boot.

"What are we gonna do?" we ask Mad Etta our medicine lady. Etta don't have to be told when there be trouble around; she smell it like a coyote smell a trap or a gun barrel.

"I worry for you," Etta say.

RCMPs mainly believe what white men tell them and like to make as much trouble as they can for us Indians. Looking for a good RCMP, Mad Etta say, is like looking out over a field of skunks for as far as you can see and trying to figure which one of the whole bunch ain't gonna make a bad smell when you get up close to it.

Every couple of days Frank Fence-post borrow Louis Coyote's pickup truck and drive Sadie up to see me. I worry some each time they do 'cause Frank don't have a driver's licence and he have to travel right up to the middle of Edmonton and even park near the police station.

One time I get to teasing Frank that he should have a good name like Ermineskin instead of Fence-post. "Ermine skins is beautiful and worth lots of money," I tell him, "while fence-posts is just dull old wood and not exciting at all."

"Fence-posts is good and real," say Frank, "I'd rather be one of them than something that don't even exist, like you."

And Frank is right, there ain't really no such thing as an ermine. I'm not sure how to put it, but it is kind of like old Miss Waits, a teacher up at the Residential School. All fall, winter and spring she is a teacher, but in the summer she ain't anything except herself. Ermines is only around in the winter, in the summer they is just plain brown weasels. Peoples a long time ago didn't even know they wasn't different animals.

In winter ermines turn to the same colour as fresh snow, all except the tip of their tail which is black and shiny like a little nugget of coal. Ermines is only about a foot long and got a body like one of them rolls of sausage that hang in butchershops. When it runs, the middle of its body bend up to make a loop like the top of a paper clip. In winter they are beautiful, in summer they is ugly. All year round they have an ugly disposition. Ermines is one of the animals that do wasteful killing. One of them will break into a hen house and kill off every single hen, just for the fun of it.

It was Frank who found Florence Rockthunder; she was just wandering around down by the highway in Wetaskiwin. Her nose be broke for sure and both eyes black and swelled almost shut. She lost too a couple of teeth from the side of her face.

"He told me he loved me," she keep saying over and over. "He said we was gonna get married so it was all right for me to tell him about his brother. He told me he didn't care about it no more."

"Did you tell him everything?"

"Everything," say Florence, spit out some blood on the floor of Mad Etta's cabin. "He was so nice to me until . . ."

"What's he gonna do?" ask Etta.

"I hear him call and ask for Constable Chretien," Florence say, "then he told Clete he'd have to wait until tonight 'cause the constable was away to Edmonton until then."

154

"So we got about six to seven hours," I say.

Florence start to cry again. "Said he wasn't gonna make the mistake his brother made of killing an ugly Indian whore."

"Be quiet," Mad Etta say to Florence. But then she look sad at her and give her a cloth, soaked in some bluish stuff been boil on the back of the stove, to hold on her face, then lay her down on the bed at the back of the cabin.

"What are we gonna do?" I say to Etta. "If Wade get to the RCMP they arrest Sadie and Florence and Bertha. And I bet Florence don't be able to keep her mouth shut. . . ."

"This is too big a medicine for me to work, Silas. I'm gonna have to try something. I only seen it once, back when I was a girl. Old medicine man named Buffalo-who-walks-like-a-man called up the Fog Spirit to help his little daughter who was awful sick. Ceremony take a long time to prepare, even though he was afraid every minute his little girl was gonna die. He boil up strong medicine that he put into bags that he tie to trees all around a small meadow. It be summer and I remember the meadow was yellow with cowslips. The fog was thick as white glue in the early morning.

"Buffalo-who-walks-like-a-man take his medicine stick and carve the shape of a woman in the fog, then there be a gust of wind even though it been still as death. That wind move off the rest of the fog and there stand the grey shape of Basket Woman, the most famous Cree medicine woman there ever was.

"She got a voice as soft as a cat walking on damp grass.

" 'Why have you called me in from the hills?' she say to Buffalo-who-walks-like-a-man.

" 'My daughter burns with a fever I cannot cure,' and he point to where little Margueretta lay on a pile of moose hides, her eyes sick and what breath she got sounding like a cat's purr. 'I have been told that if my medicine is strong

155

enough to call you here, that you do what I ask. I ask nothing for me. You can even take my life if you want it, but make my little girl better.'

" 'I will have to take her across the space between your world and ours,' Basket Woman say to the medicine man. 'Wrap her warmly in robes and bring her to me.'

"Buffalo-who-walks-like-a-man, though I bet he six and a half feet tall and have hands like bear traps, cover up his little daughter like she was made of butterfly wings and carry her to the arms of Basket Woman.

" 'You are a good man, I will do what I can,' say Basket Woman. Then she walk off across the meadow and into the scrub tamarack of the muskeg."

"What happened?" I ask.

"I'm here ain't I?" say Mad Etta, first smile, then laugh, and I notice that there be big dimples on the backs of her brown hands.

"You mean you was Margueretta?"

"Little sister of mine couldn't say my name right is how come I get called Mad Etta."

"I never knew that, I thought . . ."

"It was 'cause I was always mad at somebody?"

"Yeah," I say, which seem to get me out a lot of trouble. I guess Etta know that 'cause she waddle over to the corner and get us each a bottle of Lethbridge Pale Ale from the washtub that sit there half full of rusty water.

"Sometime I tell you what I remember of the other side."

"I'd like to hear," I say.

"I been teached the ceremony to call up the spirit of Basket Woman, but I never until now had something serious enough to use it on."

"You sure you want to use it for us?"

Etta's face get solemn as a cow's.

"You're good young people."

"You think Basket Woman would care about us? These is kind of what would be called worldly problems..."

"Basket Woman have a good heart," say Etta, and she turn her buffalo big back to indicate that the conversation is over.

Frank say that all the guys from the pool hall at Hobbema: Eathen, Robert, Rufus, Charlie and some others put together their money and call the office of Martin Prettyhand, the Indian lawyer in Calgary. Mr. Prettyhand be off to Halifax for a conference on Human Rights and stuff like that.

"We ask that when he get home he come to Edmonton to get you out of trouble," Frank say. "His secretary want to know what you been charged with, and when we tell her that they figure you might of killed a couple of white men and an RCMP she say if Mr. Prettyhand run around the country defending every Indian who killed somebody he wouldn't have time left to work on important things like Human Rights."

"I have to think about that for a while," I say.

When they leaving, Sadie always hug as much of me as she can through the bars. Sadie ain't beautiful or make a lot of laughter like Frank's girl, Connie Bigcharles, but Sadie like to kiss me, and there ain't never no doubt about how she feels about me. Sometimes when I'm loving her and we been together like one person for a long time, I look down at her face and she have her eyes closed and her face relaxed. Then she is more beautiful than Connie Bigcharles or any other girl I know. I have this tender feeling for her and it make me feel so good to know that I am the one who makes her beautiful.

I never knew Mad Etta could move so fast. She have me and Frank and Sadie stuffing wood in her stove and borrowing saucepans and when they run out gather up soup cans, and she mix up so many different kinds of stuff to boil on the stove that I don't know how she keep track of it all.

"What if Basket Woman ain't around no more?" I say. "Spirits must get old, or retire and move away to the city."

"You got a better plan you let me hear it," say Etta.

About supper time she give me some instruction that I have to pass along to Bedelia Coyote. "We can't trust Florence to help us," say Etta. "First, she ain't very smart, and second, she is hurting both inside and out right now."

Bedelia get on the phone at the Hobbema Texaco Garage and call up Wade Gaskell.

"I'm calling for Florence, she wants to see you."

I guess he ask why she don't call herself.

"Because you broke her jaw, you asshole," Bedelia yell. "All she can do is write down what she has to say. But she's still in love with you. I can't imagine why, and she says she don't tell you the whole story, whatever that means, and she wants to see you right away. She's at Wolfchild's, that's the last cabin on the right after you drive up the hill."

He must give her some more argument.

"Look, I'm just passing on a message. If you're too fucking scared to come out to the reserve then it's no skin off my nose." There is another pause.

"Like I said, I don't care whether you come or not or who you bring with you. Florence just says she has something real important to tell you." Bedelia hang up the phone.

"He'll be here," she smile. "Yellow bastards like him can't stand to be called yellow."

The car come roaring up the hill to our cabins, spreading out clouds of dust on both sides of the road. Wade is driving and his friend Clete Iverson is beside him, a shotgun poking out the passenger window. Clete is about Wade's age but is tall and thin and have red hair and a pointed face like a fox, a face that be mostly pimples and not much else.

Wade step out of the car and he is holding a sawed-off

shotgun. He look around real careful. The door to Wolf-child's cabin open real slow and while they is both looking at that I sneak from the tall grass until I'm behind the car. Then Bedelia Coyote step out of the cabin and she is wearing a red dress what was give to Sadie by a white woman one time. The dress let most of Bedelia's breasts hang out. I don't ever remember seeing Bedelia in a dress before.

"Don't point that thing at me," Bedelia say and push the gun to one side just like it was maybe a broom he was hold-ing. "Florence is laying down," she say. "You really worked her over. You know you are kind of cute. I can see why Florence likes you," and Bedelia turn and walk into the cabin wiggling her bottom at him. The shotgun is pointing at the ground as he disappear into the cabin.

I slip up the side of the car walking like I got an inch of air between me and the ground and stick the nose of my .22 right behind Clete Iverson's ear. He jump like he been poked by a cattle prod and his shotgun shoot off at the sky.

"Don't kill me, don't kill me," he say and throw his gun the rest of the way out the window. Then he put his hands on the dashboard, look at me for a second and his mouth snap shut make the same sound as closing a locker at the bus depot.

Inside the cabin Mad Etta and Bedelia got Wade tied up like he been the loser in a calf-roping contest. We tie Clete up the same way and then get busy with making up medi-cine bags, and helping Etta get dressed in her medicine woman outfit with mean paint on her face, beaded leggings and foxtails pinned all down the sleeves of her dress.

We go out to a meadow a mile or two back of the cabin and pin up the medicine bags in the trees all around so they look like tiny bird nests in the crooks of tree limbs. We also pick whatever wild flowers we can find and scatter them in a circle what Etta drawed in the lowest part of the meadow.

We are all real glad that we caught Clete Iverson 'cause it worried us how we was going to get Wade to make a telephone call. But Clete is scared whiter than he ever been before and he agree to anything as long as he figure we don't kill him. He start making the calls about nine o'clock and every fifteen minutes from then until Constable Chretien get back to his office.

"I'm out at the reserve," he explain when he finally reach the constable. "Wade's rounded up the Indians who killed his brother. He's got a gun on them and wants you out here right away. I've got to get back to help him watch them but there will be a friendly Indian meet you right by the culvert in the road and show you the way."

Bedelia and me we wrote that out on a piece of paper for Clete to say. He don't read it very good but it is enough for Constable Chretien to believe him.

I wave my hand at the RCMP car as it drive up and I'm real happy to see Constable Chretien is alone. I get in and direct him to the meadow. He ask me a lot of questions but all I say is, "White man give me $5 to meet you. I gonna buy some firewater and have a happy time. Get good and drunk," and I smile at him, stupid as I know how.

We can only get to within a hundred yards or so of the meadow. The Constable stop his car at the top of a knoll and the lights shine down into the night fog.

Constable Chretien walk slow, carry a rifle over his arm. In case we need him, Frank Fence-post is hiding off in the tall grass with a rifle of his own. I bet he is as scared as I am.

"Wade?" Constable Chretien call out.

From down in the meadow Wade answer, "Yeah, I'm down here. Everything's okay."

I don't know what Etta done to get him to say that, and I probably don't want to.

Constable Chretien let his gun point at the ground and

walk a little faster. I pick my own gun up from where it been hid in the grass, point it at him, tell him to drop his gun. Then we walk down to where Etta, Wade and Clete is. They both sit on a tree stump with their backs touching and I see that their hands ain't even tied. They both smile like the constable was just a friend what walked into the pool-hall. Boy, my whole body shakes like it twenty below and I got no shirt. I don't even want to think about how many years in jail I get for point a gun at an RCMP. I'm glad he don't know that I wouldn't shoot him. If he wanted he could just turn around and take the gun from me. We tie up his hands and sit him next to Wade and Clete. Mad Etta toss his rifle and handgun way off deep into the slough.

"Get away from here, Silas," Mad Etta say to me. "Take Frank and Bedelia too. This is my business now."

Constable Chretien's eyes be most popped out of his face and I guess he be scared too 'cause he talk a lot but mostly in French which none of us understand.

We walk back up the hill. When I turn around about half-way up I see Mad Etta holding a coup-stick which she say belong to her father, and she drawing with it what appear like the shape of a woman. Then there is a blast of wind, cold as January and the fog roll back as if it been pushed and Etta is left facing an old woman of fog, stooped in the shoulder, wearing a long dress and with a cloth covering on her head. I swing around, finish climb the hill and turn off the lights and motor of Constable Chretien's car.

I send Frank and Bedelia on by themselves and for one time they listen to me without arguing. In fact I think they glad to get away. I lean on the car and look down at the meadow.

Last I seen, there was Constable Chretien, Wade Gaskell and Clete Iverson, running off over the meadow toward a poplar grove, only I couldn't tell which one was which—

they was just three brown weasels, their eyes glowing rose-red in the moonlight, and their middles making loops like some kind of fancy handwriting, squishing together and then straightening out just like the slinky-toy my littlest sister got one time for Christmas.

It ain't long before other RCMPs come out looking for Constable Chretien 'cause he told them he was going to the reserve to meet Wade Gaskell. And Wade told somebody from town that him and Clete was coming to the reserve to meet Florence Rockthunder. We sent Florence off on the midnight bus, visit her cousins at Little Pine Reserve in Saskatchewan, and nobody around here admit there is even such a person as her. Trouble was I touched Constable Chretien's car while I was riding in it and RCMP arrest first me and then Mad Etta. They got us up here at Edmonton and since I can't explain why my fingerprints are on the car, and Mad Etta can't explain why her fingermarks was on Constable Chretien's gun what they dug out of the slough with a metal detector sound like a fast-working woodpecker, they claim we is both gonna be charged with murder.

Frank on one of his visits to me ask if there was a tiny little RCMP hat on the weasel what used to be Constable Chretien, but that kind of thing just don't seem very funny anymore.

"Have a little patience," Mad Etta tell me today, after we got to sit together in the same room waiting for RCMPs to take us to court. "It take two months before them guys come back, and when they do they'll have forgot all about us, Florence Rockthunder and Clarence Gaskell. They'll be gentle as babies. Oh, maybe they'll get a little excited when they walk past a hen house," and Etta laugh and laugh, shake like a pup-tent in a strong wind.

"What if they get killed in the meantime?" I say. "Or what if things don't work out like you planned?" Mad Etta shrug her buffalo-big shoulders.

"We're lucky it ain't trapping season," she say. "Hardly nobody shoots weasels in the summer. Hey," and she smile at me 'cause she see I'm scared. "It ain't so bad here—the grub's good and they got me a special bed 'cause when I lay on the bunk it pull right out of the wall. Have a little faith, Silas," she say and take hold of my arm with her big brown hand. "Everything's gonna be okay."

I read somewhere that faith is "believing something that nobody in their right mind would believe." I'm not sure I want to but it don't look like I got much choice.